The GNARA *Girl*

Book Two

BETTY PACK

Matchstick Literary
1-888-306-8885
orders@matchliterary.com

Prologue

Hi, everyone. My name is Rachel Cantu. I'm a nurse and hospital administrator here at All Saints Methodist in San Mateo. Texas, of course. Maybe you remember, it was my job in Book One to tell Operating Room nurse Pete Alejandro that his brother Noe had sustained an injury, gunshot wound in the back, and was being moved into immediate surgery. I was with him later, as well. As things turned out.

Nice family, tragic situation. And while I might have liked to play a much larger role in the Gnara Girl books, if not in Pete Alejandro's life, we have been just too busy with COVID at All Saints to do any lateral dating. Or going out, at all. We've had staff get sick. We've had family people upset and blaming us because they're not allowed inside to visit. One guy pulled a knife two nights ago, wanted to see his wife, we let him. We've had so many more deaths than they tell you in those constant press meetings. It takes a toll.

We employ a number of former combat medics and they say this, the stacked-up cases in the ER, hurry, hurry, is as bad as anything they experienced in Afghanistan or Iraq. I wish you could meet them, but in days ahead, in the second part of what some of us call the San Mateo Story, or we just say the 'Nara Story,' you will get to grow up and travel with the, ah, shall we say, highly energetic Gina Boswell. And, oh, Miss Lynsey, half the people in my family have worked for her, seriously. You will also find yourself curious about the motives of that butter blonde, new girl in town, Cinnah Shelton. And I promise, you'll learn more about the tender but baffling workings of men's hearts from the Sheriff, and from Preston Gerardi.

One thing. Keep one eye on Sarah Gerardi, Preston's sister. They say she's tough as nails. Secretive. Whatever. You will also meet Father Dung, really. Oh, and there's another lady I worry about, as well: Shirley Dellheim. See what you think. So, we'll be at the hospital. If you get the chance to sing, and dance, with Squad Two or the happy chef JoJo Certuche, do it. Live. Life does go on. But I'm being paged. Must run. Another day, another time, perhaps we'll meet again. For now, be well. Vaya con Dios.

Contents

Cast of Characters

Gina Boswell Greene ~ missionary and Miss Mid-Texas

Melissa & Deidra ~ Gina's grandmother and mother

Lynsey Ann ~ the journal keeper

Sarah Gerardi ~ Lynsey's police officer daughter from Houston

Preston Gerardi ~ Lynsey's 62-year-old son

Cinnah Shelton ~ butter blonde from Dell County Captain

Peter Dung ~ Vietnamese-American priest

Fausto Dellheim ~ longtime sheriff of Roeller County

Shirley Dellheim ~ Faus' wife

Yoli Guzman ~ leader of Squad Two

Magda Guzman ~ salsa dancer, singer, and member of Squad Two

Margaret "Garet" Conant ~ member of Squad Two and Louisiana girl

Dar Barush ~ Israeli electronics store owner, and speaker

Max Crawfold ~ cancer patient, master carpendar, singer of "Amazing Grace"

Jeb McMichal ~ electronics expert, American-Irish singer

The Caraman family ~ Gloria, Uncle Tony, and Aunt Andria

The Alejandro family ~ Ann, Jimmy, Pete, and the sisters

JoJo Certuche ~ Lynsey's chef and grocery shopper

Cora Emerson ~ the shooter, survivor, retired teacher

Chapter Six ~ the Girl

"Beauty is truth, and truth beauty"

Ode to a Grecian Urn

-John Keats

Gina Marie Garnier Boswell—now married, she's Gina Greene—was born a beauty. Dark lashes, big round eyes, possibly dark blue. In the next months, she kept her cute baby-smooth features, but cutest of all was the way she would pitch herself backward laughing and giggling, while held secure in some friendly adult's arms. Perhaps she wanted to overcome gravity and fly delightedly about the room, place to place, person to person. But gravity won. And soon she was standing alone, swaying this way and that, and then happily running on flat happy land through summertime sprinklers, down pathways, scattering the munching and pecking sidewalk birds, an exuberant, laughing, girly little girl. With a wild streak.

The fabulous joy Gina spread around lasted from toddlerhood until about 4th grade, thus ensuring a lingering but positive reputation would follow her into 5th grade and maybe into 6th. Perhaps a shadow of her good rep would even trail faintly behind or slightly ahead of her even into middle school, a newly attained patch considered rough by most where few kids were nice and absolutely nobody cared how cute you used to be.

But a deeper transformation had taken place during that same strange early time, somewhere mid-year, 4th grade. Like trains passing each other in the night, her joyous nature whizzed in one direction while bitter brattiness slowed, stalled, and stood parked on the opposite tracks. The result was endless moodiness. Who knew which way she would *clickety-clack* over to at what hour of which day? Instead of sharing her largesse of toys or trinkets, she insisted what was hers was hers, and don't you dare touch it. Refusing to say please and thank you, as was expected, she was all too often sent to her room, to stay. Doug and Deidra Boswell referred to Gina's punishment as "loss of perks." Gina didn't mind loss-of-perks, since she could paint her fingernails or practice putting on eyeshadow in peace and quiet. She could read her favorite magazine articles, such as the film reviews in *Time* and *Newsweek,* unusual readings for a child from a source her step-grandpa called "commie pinko rags."

Gina thought her step-grandpa was one iota above a glob of parking garage spit and her grandma Melissa was just a couple of notches above *nutso,* but interesting. She instinctively avoided Step Granddad, and he, her. But her grandmother kept a collection of saints' pictures in frames, statues of weirdo holy-holies, all sizes, and some tiny badges, and necklaces with dangling saint medallions, sort of like charm bracelets, but with holy things, not fun things. And these attracted Gina.

When she was small and still at times charming, her Melissa grandmother told her pieces and parts of ghost stories, about very young people who had died, sadly long eons ago, and so they missed out on the thrilling days of Grandma Mel's more recent yesteryear childhood when kids, all ages, roamed free, like bands of pintsize gypsies, to travel the Texas hills, free to nose around creeks and river beds like busy hummingbirds, buzzing close and closer but *seldom* flip-flapping directly into danger. "We had too much sense to get in the river and drown," her grandmother told her.

Gina remembered Grandma Mel telling her something else, more than once, as if it were a lesson Gina might forget. She told her, "There are two things about life, Gina Marie. Always be prepared to face tragedy and never forget the friends who gave you shelter when they didn't have to." Gina thought that meant, "Someday your parents will die. So you should be kind to them now." She was down with that. It made sense. Another thing rather attractive about Grandma Mel was she had tons of friends. She visited one one day, another the next day, but the best one was Mrs. Lynsey Gerardi. Sometimes Grand Mel let Gina come along when she went to see Miss Lynsey. Gina would sit with them at the big table while the old ladies drank wine from fancy glasses and talked or looked at pictures in catalogs or sometimes they sorted out old boxes of photographs and whooped and laughed or cried with their heads down on the table. Times like that, Gina would slip away to practice her dance routines on Miss Lynsey's back porch or run around the yard in wild circles as if she were an airplane or had giant-size wings. Gina liked everything about the big old house on Melody Street. Other times, alone in her room for loss-of-perks, she continued to work on her routines, really hard, not like an ordinary kid, playing around, goofing off. Her routines, her dance and cheer routines, had to be perfect, and her parents grimaced pleasantly at the sound of her thumping but distant feet and her gut-grunting high kicks. In spite of whatever Gina did to earn loss of perks, her parents were happy to drive her to her twice-weekly dance lessons. Gina was a student of tap and jazz and ballet. With permission, during middle school, when she was allowed, she began walking the five blocks after school to the dance studio, every single day, "to help out."

Once there, she would change into her ballet clothes, do a few stretches, then poke around until she bumped into some poor unnoticed little chipmunk child stuck in a class of more advanced chippers. Gina's after-school carrying ons at the studio seemed to be allowed—why not? And so, beyond her own classes, she kept showing up "to help" with the little kids. Beginning in ninth grade, she announced she had studied enough. She asked to get paid for teaching the chipmonks and was put on salary, a pittance, but salary nevertheless.

She could sing, and dance. She knew not to mouth off. She knew she looked damn good and she felt pleased with her obvious flair for getting tiny tots to jump, to leap, and not to cry, *boo hoo,* if they fell on their bottoms.

Like many out-going high school girls, Gina loved theatre, and her dream—somewhat beyond reality was to perform in or do *something* for every play, comedy show, or musical her high school produced. Every single one, if the theater teachers accepted her volunteerism, and they did, usually. But it was the acting that drove her. Besides her dance studio gig, she forced herself to try out for almost any part in every production. In four years of high school, she was one of the jealous sisters in "Xanadu," she was Rizzo in "Grease," and sweet Emily in "Our Town," a role that deeply touched Gina's heart. *We should appreciate life, but we don't—but I will,* she promised herself, *I will.*

And during her senior year, Gina was Maria in "West Side Story." To prove she was a good sport, even when she got passed over for a part, she branched out backstage, lifting scenery, sorting costumes, even doing make-up. Clean-up was not above her station. She strove to be there—every single time—to set up and tear down. Some people in San Mateo predicted a great future for Gina and hoped one day soon they would see her—her legs sensuously crossed perhaps—talking in a know-it-all voice, probably on Fox News. Just as Gina's fourth grade moodiness/sassiness had come upon her, as time grew closer to the end of her secondary education, her dirty moods lifted. Finally free of pouts-and-fits and a general all-round cussedness, she became serious. Deathly serious. Every summer Gina had been used to helping out at Vacation Bible School, but it was only for a week of kicks and giggles, and flirtations with the boys her age also volunteering with VBS. But now she took it upon herself to sign up to be a helper with the second grade holy communion classes at church *every Sunday morning*. She talked her mother into it by claiming how easy it would be since she already knew some of the "kiddy-pies," as she now called them, from dance classes. While pondering if she could also start doing once-a- month readings at the Sunday evening teen mass, she applied for and was given a real job at a serious agency that provided sitters for the aged and elderly. It was called Jitterbug—a name that caused Gina to fear they were going to make old people get up and boogie, but it was all good. Gina was up for it because, remember, she used to help little kids learn to dance. If she had to dance with old people, Ok. It just sounded weird. But she did want the job, she wanted to be around old people. She was going to write a play about their lives. Maybe turn it into a musical. And while it was legal in Texas for a child, beginning at 15, to work a few hours after school, Gina, at 16, thought she could visit Jitterbug's clients until at least 2100 hours. She never went to sleep before midnight anyhow. And was never tired.

The owners of the company thought she could do office work. Gina at Jitterbug, then, sat at a desk, answered the phone, checked schedules as a reminder of which sitter was, at any time, with which client. Gina was *gung ho*, that's what her step-grandpa said about her—"Gina is 'gung ho' to get whatever she wants"—and what she wanted was to get to know the sitters, the workers at Jitterbug, who usually appeared at the office during the same after-school hours she was at her desk. She struggled to make her ears stand up and hear whatever the sitters said about their clients.

These sitters, most of them, were about the age of her mother, and Gina couldn't help but compare them with Deidra Boswell. The thing is, Deidra didn't hit it off with old-old people. No, Gina's mom was a consumer. And, as if to prove they were a match made in heaven, Gina's dad, a worker, was a man of means. In high school, Gina wondered once or twice if her parents still had sex and when, but she didn't want to know. One day, she had a flash of realization: *I'm more like Dad than Deidra.* "Why?" She asked herself why because, while it hurt and upset her to admit it, she really liked Deidra better. Deidra was a sweetie, but an absolute pain. Like Grandma Mel, she was almost some kind of bird, innocently flapping around her. No, Deidra was a sad, teasing hummingbird, flapping, flapping, then backing away.

Saturday mornings, traipsing off to the dance studio to help out and later to teach the tiny dancers, Gina recognized children as total fun. They made her smile. She almost laughed at the very idea; but she identified with the little thumb suckers, and the *panty line pickers*, the whiners and weepers who would rather be home with their toys. Teachers were not allowed to hug the children, but Gina had a way of scrunching down, hovering over a tiny grump, offering a temporary covering, a metaphysical hand to hold, and the advice to "Get over it."

That was Gina's Saturday morning. Building up her little kiddy-pies. Wowser. How *fun*. Afternoons might mean play practice, oh, those never-ending rehearsals. At times, she had to cut back at Jitterbug and at dance because school and theater came first. Even so, she was usually at her Jitterbug desk every afternoon until seven o'clock, when the state of Texas says employees under age 18 need to go home and rest.

She began to beg to go out on visitations with the sitters, Ok, she didn't beg. She simply asked why, like, couldn't she just string along with someone, be a sitter's helper or assistant? Gina had found that if she asked Deidra, over and over, to be allowed to do, or buy, whatever she wanted, her mother would soon give in and say Ok, do or buy whatever you want. Gina told the sitters, women her mother's age, "I won't be any trouble. I'll just string along and be your assistant, and I have my own car, so I can leave whenever I want, around seven." That little *I-have-my-own-car-at-age-16-and-will-leave-when-I-want* song-and-dance might not have been the best thing to say to someone who, at 40, has yet to own a car of her own, but Gina had much to learn. Not one sitter invited her to be an assistant, to string along. Not one. Time passed.

Those employed as sitters could travel to sit with clients in their own cars, and claim mileage, or they could use one of the pre-owned Jitterbug Smart Cars Preston bought at auction. Gina thought, *Oh, Ok, that's fine, it's all good, as long as I get what I want.* And so she started watching for someone really malleable, some sweetheart willing to take her along, like, let's see, someone her mother's age who would really be able to understand why Gina likes to be around old people, needs to listen to them, to learn things, someone who'd treasure and respect Gina's various abilities. She narrowed her selection process down to one woman. A pretty woman.

When Gina made her new approach, in private, in a warm tone of voice, she confided to the pretty sitter, "What I really want you to do is just let me go with you to see the old people—I'll drive because I have to leave at seven but I bet you can get someone to pick you up wherever you are, end of your shift. And I'm asking *you* because you remind me of my mom and, well, I just want to sit with the elderly and just listen to them because I plan to write a play about the lives and troubles of old people. For my Advanced Placement English class."

The sitter looked at her hard enough, long enough, to make Gina's heart go flip-flop. But the sitter told her, in a soft voice, that she was not her *mom* and if she were, she would knock Gina's head off, that she would not be driven by Gina anywhere on this earth and then be dumped somewhere, not only no, but hell no, and if Gina thinks she has the right to make a school skit out of the lives and troubles of old dying people, then she better turn in her resignation this very day, or the sitter would happily do it for her, and she might just tear Gina's head off for the fun of it, and for Gina to stay the hell away from her.

Time passed. Gina told no one about her encounter with the pretty sitter. She was embarrassed, and annoyed with herself. She waited. Kept to herself. One afternoon in the Break Room, Julie, one of the sitters Gina had once asked about letting her "string along," inquired of Gina if she still wanted to visit clients instead of sitting by the phone. Gina said, "Yes, but—" and threw her hands up, Deidra style, in dismay and despair.

Julie said, "Hon, you need to get over it—that thing about writin' a play, oh, no, no. You need to ask the owners." And that would be Preston Gerardi or the real owner, his mother, Lynsey Gerardi. Gina was shocked, and jubilant. And humbled. *Get over it.* Of course—and the owner, *yes.* Of all things, Mrs. Gerardi was Gina's special own old friend from childhood. "How stupid I am, stupid in a hundred ways," she said and stayed home sick from school the next morning so she could privately call and made an appointment with Mrs. Gerardi. For the earliest day possible. Gina didn't like to wait.

Miss Lynsey remembered Gina and told her rules were meant to be broken, about going outside the box, against the tide. Sometimes. Some rules. Asinine rules. Some boxes. Mental boxes. Some tides. *Neap* tides. "N-e-a-p, look it up, if you're hankering to know when to go, when to stop, which rules to break." Gina was struck silent. Adults usually tried to persuade Gina into agreeing to follow all rules.

Every rule. This tall, kind of spooky old lady said strange things, that was for sure. She had a way of making ordinary life questionable and mysterious. Lynsey told her, "I was about your age when I started sitting, first with my great aunt. You've likely heard the story. I slept on the floor next to her bed. People said I should stop, that I was too crazed with grief over the, ah, passing of my mother. And I was. I was plenty *loco, loca, plenty crazy*, and not only because of my mother. But if I had listened to what people said and stopped caring for my aunt, what would have happened to her? I loved her dearly, you see, but what if she had been horrible, a wretched person? If she'd been in diapers and routinely messed on herself, what if she screamed all day for loved ones who never came, never could. Tell me, what would you do?" She fell silent, as they say. And waited.

"Then," Gina said, slowly, not—for once in her life—certain, "then I guess I might try to start something like Jitterbug, only I would call it *Tango*, and I'd bring in children, little volunteers, with their parents' permission, of course, and puppies, and I wouldn't mind cleaning up after them, but puppies make people happy, or I can sing, I could maybe sing for them. Or *with* them. Maybe."

"Now, then," Lynsey said after a considerable pause, "I am told you want to make visitations, and that you have your own transportation. You have your own car at sixteen, Ok *seventeen*. As it should be. Why not? You're legal. So, you may, as far as I am concerned, go with anyone willing to take you, *one* day a week—somebody else can answer the phone, or I will—if you promise me to leave at seven, so we don't get thrown in jail, *alrightee*? Is that a deal?"

"Yes, *ma'am*, it's a deal," Gina said, all but jumping up to hug her. This was wonderful—it was exactly what she wanted. What a grand lady.

The grand lady reminded Gina, "*Seven* PM. At your age, Texas law says you must stop 'working' and be gone by seven o'clock but you could visit someone, your grandmother every day—but no, I have loved your grandmother for countless years, so no, no. No nursing home for our Melissa. Let's say instead you visit an *uncle* or a retired teacher at the local nursing home, and you stay until nine o'clock at night? There would not be a peep, not one peep, out of anybody. But because you are working to put bread on your family's dinner table, so to speak, you must leave at seven. Do you see, my dear? Our laws are perfectly imperfect."

A smiling Gina agreed. Thereafter she was just wild about Miss Lynsey Gerardi—almost as if she had a crush on her. But wait. She still had to find someone to accept her, but who? How? She waited. Time passed.

When their paths crossed, which was not often because Miss Lynsey sometimes felt poorly—it was, most likely, in the Jitter Break Room, a cool place with cold drinks, and coffee, and junk food machines, and tables and chairs. Words rolled around the room when the boss sat with her people, free words and open-ended discussions. They welcomed and included everyone, even applicants looking for work. Around that time, a new hairstyle was making the rounds of insider half-celebrities and outsider machinists, miscreants, and motorcycle gang members. Perhaps the hairstyle was created as some dubious half-salute to Britney Spears when, a few years into adulthood, an emotional meltdown caused her to shave her own head completely bald. It, this "hot" new hairdo, was called "the partialy shaved head," or "the half-shaved hairstyle." Women with long, often beautiful, hair went into salons of their own free will and chose to offer one side of their head to the clippers, the buzzsaw, the blade. One Saturday AM when the dance studio was closed because the older students and teachers were away at competition, Gina waltzed deliberately and happily into a San Mateo salon and submitted her head to the half-shaved hairstyle.

Her parents said nothing about the loss of half of Gina's silky and shining long brown hair. Deidra wondered briefly if she ought to run to the salon to claim her daughter's crowning glory, save some of the curls. She was frightened for her girl; going to school like that, what with the way kids are so mean today—that almost threw Deidra into a tizzy, and she considered phoning Sheriff Dellheim but nothing or nobody had overtly threatened her headstrong, half-bald only child. Not yet. All she could do was to hope. *Hope.* She would *expect* the best, the best protection, as she had prayed all weekend and cringed in fear that Sunday night as thunder boomed, lightning flashed and heavy rain drenched Mid-Texas. She worried that Gina might drive into a low-water crossing and get trapped. Although the farmers and gardeners needed rain, she prayed for it to stop and for Gina to safe all day Monday.

That Monday morning, back at school, First Period, 7:55 to 8:45, Gina was, as usual, steeled and unmoved by the catcalls, the testing scorn of the Mean Girls, the jeers, boos and hisses aimed at no less than the whole of civilization.

Blame it on lack of sleep, most of the teenage students having been awake until—or since—three or four AM, and not because of the still-booming rain storm. They were just grumpy, tired, resentful, dry little matches, willing wicks, waiting for someone to burst them into flame. Unfortunately, this little scholastic "watch out for me, I am in a bad bad-mad mood" presentation was expected, even permitted, at some American high schools. Gina's classmates, some she had known since kindergarten, were now settling into a sullen leave-me-alone alternative mood.

They were sending by special delivery the message no teacher left unread: Just you be careful—I might be suicidal. Yes or no, some regularly considered punishing those close to them to be fair game. Word of anything interesting was *slow, yo mama,* but by the end of Third Period, the same old kids were gearing up for action, any kind of action. Sleepyheads were shoving smaller students, tripping girls they knew lacked the nerve to complain or who would take the attention as approval, evidence of a flirtation.

Sexy seniors, as some 12th grade male students were allowed to call themselves, were sending winks and nods and certain quick gestures toward young or insecure teachers as they stood at the opened doors of their classrooms, arms folded, doing change-of-class duty to oversee and prevent "incidents" in the halls.

Suddenly, over the PA system, three bells chimed, and one of the office secretaries announced, "Students, students, all classes to-*day* will be shortened"—*whistles and cheers*—"by seven minutes"—*boos and groans*—"and students will be given an extra seven minutes between classes because of the rain and the mud from these rain storms and because *some* students in the portable classrooms have been having mud fights, all students will now walk to their other classes using only the regular and designated walkways and should not cut across the landscape, tearing up flower bed and tracking mud into the main buildings."

Gina had been on the down-low all morning. She was aware, she thought, of the consequences of getting her head shaved. She would look funny for a while, but an attractive, nay, a pretty girl, can always make a negative in her appearance turn into a plus for her personality. Deidra worried too much, but not *that* much, since she couldn't even get out of bed this morning and make poor Gina any breakfast. *Mothers.*

Anyway—what do they say—"pretty girls work harder." Gina knew that was true. Nobody had to invite her twice or had to waste time pulling her out of a shell. She cared for, and respected, other people so much that she would perpetually meet them more than halfway. She was joyful, outgoing, generous and kind to all. It wasn't difficult. If you are nice and bubbly around people, they will always admire and like you.

Being pretty was fun; it was all plus-plus. At first, over the weekend, Deidra's worried face (for once in her life her parents had left her to sleep in; didn't even call her to go to church with them) had scared Gina. But she could handle people, and that Monday morning had arranged her half-hair in a flattened circle around her skull and sprayed and pinned it into place. She had dressed herself to seem somber and sedate, mixing blacks and browns together, and fixing an ugly old olive green scarf at her neck. If she had been interviewed she would laugh lightly and just say it was what she thought of as her Parisian look. Poor Deidra, nothing to worry about. This was going to be *fun*.

At the end of 3rd period, following the directions of adding seven minutes between classes—and next up was her lunch period, when she didn't even really *need* to eat—she took time to visit the *Girls* and to patiently wait for her turn at the mirror. She patted her hair. Still in place. Maybe tomorrow she'd wear it down and around to *show* her more timid classmates. All morning she'd been deliberately quiet, acting so very sophisticated, and so so weary with all that was high school, this ridiculous Audie Murphy High School in San Mateo, ridiculous Texas. How tedious.

She smeared a snappy coral lipstick on her lips, smacked them together. *Lookin'* good, she thought and then noticed a ring of girls watching her, and by the time she stepped out into the cafeteria courtyard, word was out. An assumed friend had taken on the role of Gina Bosewell's teenage life critic and judge: Named Dustin Hawkins. His gang of three or four ungrown men were suddenly and inexplicably out for revenge. By instant action, Dustin's followers soon expanded and everyone in the courtyard was pushing and shoving, tearing at her hair, her bosom, her dignity. Gina, dizzy from the slaps and punches, looked around, calling for help. No one came to help her.

Allen Plesalla, a kid never on any team, never won an election, although his parents thought he should, grabbed her from behind, his hands on her breasts, and screamed into her ear, "Why don't you go put on shorts and a top where you let it all hang out, ya whore, ya slut!"

Collin Thomas, a guest at every one of Gina's birthday parties since the were both four, let his bottom jaw slip forward and whined, "My brother ain't gonna ask you to the prom now. By the way, my parents *hate* you, you hairless bitch."

A member of the student council arrived, and there was a brief pause in the action because he, nameless here, was known for his leadership and integrity. He smiled, and was cheered by name. He waved for quiet and, pulling at his chin hairs, said, "Hey, Gina. I used to defend you, but with this new look, you really look like white trash, and that is what you are!" He was cheered yet again. Reaching carefully into his messenger bag, he gloated and teased, pulling out one, two, three, *four* paper drink-cartons. He announced, "I've got *mud*."

Dustin Hawkins merely said, "Yay, *mud*, pass it around." Then he shouted at Gina: "See there, nobody likes you, Miss Works-With-Kids, works-with-old-farts. I bet they fire your ass. Nobody wants you around. *Nobody*."

Gina just stood, saying nothing as kids, her classmates, pushed and shoved to get a handful of mud. They passed it around, like sacred food, and began pelting her with it and chanting: *"Mud on Gina, mud on Gina, mud on Gina."*

Gina still stood, silent, dodging mud, protecting her face, her eyes, when two things happened: the drug dogs arrived and another voice boomed, like a thunderbolt: *Knock it off, you guys. Stop bullying her! Where're you supposed to be? Go, walk!*

Gina didn't recognize the voice, but kids began to pick tell-tale spots of mud off their clothes as teachers and the vice principal closed in along with the drug dogs, and their handlers. Watchers, onlookers, might claim the vice principal broke up the unruly hate-crowd, but it was the voice, the unrecognized voice, *and* the dogs. The drug dogs.

Lean and sturdy as ponies, draped in leather cords and plastic-wrapped ID cards, the powerful rumbling, slobbering dogs pulled on their leashes, making their keepers lean in as the dogs, observant creatures, in an act of animal excellence, a moment of empathy, *spak thusly* in their own voices, to each other. For those who could hear, the dogs spoke in English. Some kids—ones perhaps with amiable hearts—heard some of the words. Some heard no words. Gina heard them all:

Mutt, a ninety-pound Alsatian wolf dog, muttered: *Hey, hounds. What's been going on here?*

Pup Pup, shaking with energy, spoke in a scary voice: *Looks like we need to tear somebody's britches to pieces. And guess who I see?*

Mutt: *Yeah, that Dustin brat. I think we might have to take him down. What if we break loose and go for that whole crowd near the little bitch.*

Miss Whiskers, a Pit Bull Terrier with a cat's name, disliked combat or anything that might tear up her precious coat, but she purred at the male dogs. *"Ok, but how do you know the bitches from the studs?*

Pup Pup laughed, *Aw, the fat round ones are bitches and the studs look old and tired, from all the drugs.*

Miss Whiskers wanted to know, *What about that one, the bitch they're fixing to kill?*

Spanner, an old dog, a fierce and still fast Doberman rumbled, *You young dogs. They're not going to kill her, they just want to torture her. She looks like somebody already took a bite outta her head, but I like her. Tell ya, if that Dustin bastard touches her, I'm callin' free game, no rules, let him have it. Ready?*

Pup Pup: *Now wait! When I say, when I give the signal, Spanner, then we'll bust out of these straps. Whisker, you stand guard. Mutt, go straight for Dusty boy. Make him cry for momma. Spanner? You're with Mutt. I'll weave in and see if the dirty bitch will run with me an' hop into the back of the truck. Stay the course with me now and when every last human is crying and whining, we are outta here, headin' for the hills.*

Dustin Hawkins, aware of the dogs, hearing their threats, felt the icy fear of dog-doggies he'd had since toddlerhood. Today he had made a mistake, lost his mojo. With no lunch, his tum-tum rumbled, and he was filled with dread over what might come next, after drug dogs. The cops? He'd only wanted Gina to notice him, be *his* prom date. Slinking away, old Dusty did the easiest thing available: He left the courtyard for the anonymity of the hallways of his public high school. And as for Gina, she knew the drug dogs and the *voice* were blessings and she felt grateful and when students came to her later and said, "Sorry, Gina, we apologize for them, will you be Ok?" she told them, "Hey, it's all good."

The attack on Gina Bosewell, early October, 2011, same time as Occupy Wall Street protests filled the daily, hourly news, lasted less than the extra seven minutes allowed, but it changed a life, several lives. In a gathering knot of students trying to comfort Gina, two or three girls cried. Some, angry with the unknown, felt lost and confused. How had this happened? Here, at their school? It was like Hitler. *That day some of them began to say 'never again' over and over to each other.* Gina, being escorted to the counselors office, waved to the drug dogs. "Bye, bye, you sweetie-pies, love you," she said. All this, the pity, the mud balls, hearing animals speak, imagining that other voice, made her reek of strangeness all day, and guilt. She promised herself, "I don't want to be different," and in her mind she now knew being different can kill you. Refusing the chance to go home early, she left school at the regular time, a teary-eyed mess— carefully driving *where?* Home to get-down with Deidra, cry and moan, hug and rock, eat everything yummy in the house and watch romantic comedies? While an evening of yummies and rom-coms appealed, she turned the other way. Face the music. See if Dustin was right. Would she be fired? Never to visit the elders.

When Lynsey Gerardi called for her to drop everything and come to her office, Gina was scared senseless. *Knock, knock.* Since Lynsey was not a hugger, not known to be physically affectionate, she had something else in mind for Gina. People had told her about what had happened at school; they were concerned, but Miss Lynsey had the girl turn this way and that, and said, "Very cute. Now sit down and relax. Actually it's very dashing. The two sides of Gina, one bold and daring, a bit muddy, and the other more traditional. I'm told today was tough for you," Lynsey said, "but you'll only get stronger, you will."

"I didn't think people would be so mean," Gina said, "that's what scares me."

Lynsey nodded, "Tragedies happen, but remember friends will also be there. You know, if I could, I would go get my head shaved like yours, except all my life I have been stuck with my side-by-side companions, reticence and caution. R and C. I have traveled, been a cautious tourist here and there, always staying on the bus."

She gestured toward a tennis-ball-shaped blue and green earth intended for its owner to squeeze to counteract carpal tunnel syndrome or numb fingers. "I have not touched the earth, Gina, I have only connected with home plate, here in San Mateo, but not you.

"You will go places, you well squeeze this earth, and I want you to know you will have my full support wherever you go, and that's why I want you to have *this*," and Lynsey slowly removed a jade ring from her own finger and offered the ring to the stunned teenager.

"No, really?" Gina gushed, "Oh, how pretty," and slipped the ring on her finger. "Thank you, a million times."

"Wear it," Lynsey said, "put it in a box, hang it on a chain around your neck or on a lamp post, but keep it. Now go back out there with your head high. Hair grows back. People forget. But, *erm*, you might go find Julie Rosen. She wants to see you about going along on visits."

And so time passed. Gina's spirits healed and took flights. She worked her Jitter job consistently and loved her visits with the elderly. Her hair grew back. She chopped off the other side. It began to even out, and she soon realized she'd been at Jitter for a year and a half and had been making visits for three months, for two to three hours twice a week. She had learned that sometimes waiting for what you want can be just the ticket. Although Miss Lynsey was ancient, she knew things, and Gina had questions, and she liked to talk, get into discussions where she used some of her favorite sayings such as "All things are relative," and "same-same," and especially, "It's all good." One sunny day, Lynsey, was resting in the Break Room, when she called out to Gina, "Come on over, it's time we have a natter." Gina looked hurt. "You mean like a fight," she asked, and Lynsey explained, "No, like a *chat*." With Gina folding away a new word, they began.

The pace was slow, deliberate. Lynsey queried the girl, first nonchalantly, asking her how Gina's parents were. The teenager wrinkled her nose and said, "Same-same, it's all relative with them." When Lynsey asked if Gina would mind explaining what she had just said, Gina told her, "Sure, 'It's all good' means no worry, you haven't hurt my feelings or done anything bad, because, well, everything is just *good*. And 'all things are relative' means, like, we should all be brothers and sisters, no difference, and 'Same-same' is just saying we're all equal."

"*Pshaw*, girl, you ought to live in New Orleans. Your parents don't ever take you to New Orleans, the Big Easy? It's so close, but get off the bus. Ok, Ok, I said that because your attitude, your little sayings—peace on earth, good will to men—reveals a *laissez-faire* mindfix. Looesy-goosey, you see?

"You like *le Francaise*? You do. You, my dear, would like to roll around in *joie de vivre*. Not the perfume but in the absolute joy of life. Gina thought of Emily in *Our Town*, and frowned.

Years later, in India, in trouble in India, Gina remembered Miss Lynsey making her think about how what we say, over and over, gets under our skin, into our minds, and can become the creeping motive behind our actions.

Lynsey told her, "Don't fall for the theory of relativity. In science it's popular, then it's not popular. It depends. I'm talking about real life, about choices, and about how you must use your power of judgment and discernment."

With things, with people, with actions, Gina realized, it's not all good, not relative. It is not the same-same here as there-there. And to mindlessly say, to try to believe, that all things are good denies reality. Gina knew, even if yet to understand, that there are absolutes. Truths. Facts. Some things are, after all, unchangeable, almost as if they were carved in stone. Gina had a lot to think about.

~~~

Just weeks before high school graduation, Gina was working the phones in the Jitterbug outer office and waiting room. Oddly enough, she was beginning to like manning the phones. She was just ending a call when she noticed Mrs. Gerardi seated in a comfortable plump fake-leather chair. Unusual. But whatever. And then, from across the room, as if speaking to an audience, Lynsey shouted, "Avoid pointed toe shoes like the plague." Some people were startled and at first thought the boss was yelling at them. "It's just that Gina and I were talking about shoes a while back"—Gina blinked in surprise—"and I have noticed every day I have to ask myself am I 78 or 87? Some people, *secret* people, might say, 'You are one or the other, just don't start telling the same stories again.' Some guy might ever tell me to zip it, my mouth, that is."

Faces were turned toward her. Sitters, applicants, cleaning ladies. Inspectors. Men who'd come to service the snack machines. They were listening; a few seemed to be alarmed. Lynsey shouted, "If he did that, we might ask him if he zipped up his zipper, but never mind him; this is about *you*, and we do love men." Some ladies giggled. And Gina felt her face burning. She ducked her head.

"Here are some tips," Lynsey announced to one and all, "just some tips to keep in mind as you age, and aging isn't bad, no, no. Now there are two things I need to share with you, and you gentlemen, tell your wives, your sisters, your friends. If you pretty young ladies want to preserve your bodies and looks and good health into old age, such as the eighties, never wear flip flops. Don't throw them at your children, *ha ha*.

"Funny thing about the flying *chancla*. Flip flop, I mean. Did y'all know there's a baseball team called Flying Chanclas? Yay, you *know!* I had to read about it in the newspaper, but if you don't know, here it is: The idea came from how mommas have eyes in the back of their head, right? You know, the kid's on the other side of the room, tell me if it's like this—and he keeps messing with something. Let's just say he is teasing the cat, again. He's been told one hundred times to leave that cat alone. She's going to scratch him to pieces. So, there he is, once again, annoying the cat, looking around, doing it again, and then suddenly, sailing across the room, the flying chancla—and *WHAP!* Yay, for the Mexican, very American, mother with perfect aim. A sailing, flying flip flop right upside the *cabeza,* the noggin, of this former and now retired cat-torturer." Lynsey managed a half smile, took a deep breath. Gina sat down at her desk. She was worried.

Lynsey continued. "*Whew,* may that poor old cat live many lives. No, ladies and gentlemen, I say no flip flops, because if you wear flip flops all day long, you're on your feet, and chances are, after a while, your arches and heels are going to start barking. That's why they call your feet *dogs*. No, buy and wear the best shoes you can afford, because the real pain starts later on with damage to the spinal system. Y'all ever heard this song, c'mon sing it with me, s-shake it, '*The ankle bone's* connected to the leg bone and the leg bone's *connected to —what?—to the knee bone, an' the leg bone—*"

Gina was near tears. What should she do? Go get Miss Lynsey a cold drink and try to distract her? Go look for Mr. Preston and tell him *what?* That his mother's singing?

Lyns' Ann and a handful of listeners were getting into it, again, anew, "...*the leg bone be connected to de knee bone, de knee bone's done connected to the' thigh bone*—"

Gina waited, afraid to death that the elderly and possibly lost owner of Jitterbug was getting louder. "Don't panic," she told herself, and at last the song was over.

Lynsey shouted, "Ladies, take care of your teeth. Keep your same dentist, if possible, and over time your fees will build a deck on that rascal's house, buy his kids their first car. Your feet, and teeth." And then she paused. She put a hand on her face. "I apologize," she said. "Dear friends, I am talking like a privileged old silly white woman. I am a sorry thing. But somehow in this country, this—our ability or inability—to get dental care has got to change. Listen. There are so many beautiful ladies who can't can't afford the dentist, money goes for the kids, for bills, until she's in pain and he says gotta pull that tooth. Damn those dentists," Lynsey shouted, holding onto the arm of a woman who had reached out to her. "Damn them when you see a beautiful woman with a missing tooth and she can't talk or even smile without revealing her loss. Damn, damn, damn, you dentists—she can't even *chew* her food—greedy mongrel dogs."

Gina was stunned. When she looked up, Mr. Preston was leaning on the wall outside his office, arms folded. Gina was a bit nearsighted (at 17, she considered it her only physical flaw) but was Mr. P smiling? He looked so fierce most of the time. And had he just *winked* at her? Lynsey was standing flat-footed, arms raised. She went for her finale: "You dentists are obliged by justice. *Fix her tooth.* A missing tooth is a gaping wound to the soul. To the spirit. You call yourself *doctor*, no way, bunch of bloody bastards, I tell ya."

Gina had never heard Miss Lynsey talk like that, had never thought about the *why* behind missing teeth. And Mr. Gerardi? In about an hour, he sent Gina a message to drive his mother to the house on Melody Street.

That night Gina helped Deidra straighten the house, did her homework, picked out totally beige and khaki clothes for the next day and when she went to bed, she cried for a long time.

Time passed, and while Gina reluctantly agreed to attend Baylor University, her parents' first choice, she was elated by the theater arts program. She and her parents agreed that theater would be her major. Gina committed herself to college, becoming a serious student, staying at Baylor, reviewing her notes, not coming home, except when they closed the doors of the on-campus residence where she shared a room with a seriously Baptist girl from Alabama. Gina liked Heather, the roommate.

She felt comfortable at Baylor, was awed by the lavish and seriously mature drama productions her theater department produced, several each semester. Gina had danced and had sung her heart out in a couple of musical reviews for after-the-show ticket holders who wanted just a little more entertainment before going out to play in highway traffic. She had one short speaking part in one of the plays produced in a series of five short plays. But she enjoyed it all and, aside from her part in her own short play, she "learned" the words of each of the three other short plays, just in case she had to fill in.

The overall theme of these short plays was sadness and loss and how to live with it. Gina thought she could relate, but she knew she had only second-hand losses, borrowed sorrows. Yet she suffered. When she passed a broken-down car and saw others daring to stop and help, she teared up. When she offered a hug to the broken-hearted girl three doors down who was dumped by her boyfriend in an unnecessarily cruel fashion, she *felt* it. Gina loved to help, to fix things, to stop the pain by crashing in, with open hands, open heart. And, well, open mouth.

She knew her heart, her own life, was racing into the unknown. While she was at Baylor, Gina first found the cool taste that seemed to quench a deep dry thirst, a thirst she could only describe as a need to leap—a *jeté*—into the historical race of discovering and mastering, and deeply living, *true* faith. She longed to be a missionary. A Catholic missionary at a Baptist school, she needed to make some choices and take some deliberate steps toward her future without forgetting the lessons of the past. She was 18-going-on-19, so her parents placed two stipulations on Gina's urge to "get religious" and go to Belize or perhaps Canada to do her missionary work. She must wait, number one, until after her sophomore year to become a missionary and, number two, in the intervening 12 months, she must enter and prepare to win the Miss Texas beauty pageant. "Not a problem," Gina assured them. Not a problem at all.

During this same period of time, her parents arranged for Gina to be in the right place at the right time and to meet many attractive and eligible young men. Gina went out with every fellow who asked her, at least once. She tried to set aside time for these go-nowhere dates. Her intention was only to prove kindness still exists. You asked me out, and waited patiently, until I was home from Baylor, and so I will be your date in San Mateo, at least once. She had great fun during this period of her own generosity. She enjoyed being liked, it seemed, by everyone on earth as she prepared for both the pageant and for her new life as a missionary.

End of her second year at Baylor, Gina had won her local pageant and was entitled to parade around as Miss Middle Texas, wearing a tiara and a sash that spelled out, "Miss Mid-Texas 2013." This caused confusion for some people who thought the sash meant she was already the official Miss Texas, all set and ready to compete for the title of Miss America or Miss USA. One or the other. Gina told her mother and her supporters, not to worry. Those poor little souls just don't read well.

To celebrate and help build up her self-confidence, Gina planned a trip to New York city—as opposed to New York state, although, honestly, the state appealed to Gina more than did the city. But she smiled gamely and tagged her four-day excursion as "my hit-the-*road* trip," waited twenty seconds and asked, "Get it? *Road* trip? Hit the Road? *Trip?*" When people asked if she would be talking with Fox News or trying out for some off-Broadway play, Gina just smiled and said, "Yes, ma'am," or "No, sir," whichever was most appropriate.

Upon her return to San Mateo, her parents asked her to go to her room—that same room, redecorated—because they discovered that, while in New York, Gina had spent considerable time at the Indian Embassy. "*Indian* Embassy," her parents shouted almost in unison. "What do you think you were doing at the Indian Embassy?" her dad asked and her mother asked, "What do you think you were doing? At the Indian Embassy?"

"Mostly waiting," she told her father. "Getting acquainted," she told her mother. "I am moving to India."

"We thought you were going to be a missionary," her dad yelled. Deidra screamed, "Don't you realize you should be getting ready for the actual big-time Miss Texas pageant *in two weeks?"*

Gina began ignoring her parents' questions and comments although she did confide to several puzzled pals that, yes, soon she was leaving San Mateo to be a missionary in India.

Word got around to her devastated parents who nonetheless cheered their daughter through pageant week and consoled her when she was instantly eliminated *after* the swimsuit competition because Gina, who was beautiful, charming, who tap-danced adequately and flattered the judges, had, at the very last minute, refused to wear the required two-piece (almost string) pageant bikini. Instead, waiting in line to show some skin, she stripped buck naked and pulled on a different swimsuit, one she had found stored with her mother's supply of old or unused clothing. It was a still-bright canary yellow, a 1950s Jantzen one-piece suit, Esther Williams style, with an actual belt of the same fabric that cinched Gina's waist to look inches smaller than her bare-middled sister contestants. The color flattered her flowing dark hair—half of it piled high—and her green eyes, but an uproar was at hand as the suit came almost *up to her chin* and covered her *entire* bottom.

Mr. and Mrs. Boswell, who sometimes secretly asked each other if Gina might have a mental illness, were simply stupefied. Mr. B muttered to his wife, "Let's just get the hell back to the hotel," but Mrs. B, Deidra, silent as a stone, seemed to be smiling around the edges. As parents nonsensically enamored with their own child, they forced themselves to cheer Gina on, even as she left Texas to be a missionary in India. She stayed three years.

The first year, she was disappointed not to be assigned to work in the field, to be with the Catholic *tribes*, the indigenous peoples of India. That's what she had signed up for, but they told her she needed to learn about the overall culture of India first, so she worked in a school for children ages 6 to 10, helping them to read English and master English grammar. During quiet time she talked with them about their composition topics, but she kept asking permission to work with the nearby tribes, gradually moving up the chain, asking the next one up, when would she be assigned to the tribes?

One day Gina mentioned to another missionary, a woman of about 40 from Canada, who wore a scarf hanging down the back of her head, that the kids in her classes already spoke better English than she did. The Canadian grinned and told Gina no, not true, because you don't really speak English, you speak Texan. Gina wasn't sure how to take that but she was tempted to ever so lightly pull the old gal's headpiece off and say, "Ooo, my bad, I seemed to have pulled your pajamas off." But, no, that would be harsh, so Gina just grinned and waited her turn with the tribes. She was determined—she had grown up with the profound American message: Follow your dreams, there's no limit, nothing is beyond you if you really want it—but she had learned recently that the virtue of patient waiting and gracious silence can come in handy. At times.

Back in Waco, when Gina was still at Baylor University, a story had made the rounds, scaring the whiskers off of everyone taking speech and drama classes or planning a career in radio or television. It went like this: An extremely attractive, well-brought up, much-travelled young man, educated at Boston University or the University of Florida, take your pick, was determined to get what he wanted: Star treatment and an early-on prime assignment to headline the evening news. His credentials were excellent on paper, on video. In person, he was number one. But impatience and pride pushed him ahead of himself. Through certain well-considered machinations—being a top skeet shot, an actual "Ted" talker, a prize-winning "highway poet," a second-place winner at the "distinguished young film editor" tournament, and placing among the top ten in the national "old time golf" challenge—he sought out and charmed his way into parties and events featuring the station owners and their milieu, but not as a guest. No, what our young man did was this: He began to work his way—as a volunteer—through the social world of his bosses, as a volunteer waiter, complimentary bar man, surprise event greeter and snappy valet parking attendant. Short of marrying the boss's daughter, he would soon be so necessary, so very well known, so deeply liked, that he could easily slide into the news slot he so coveted.

So, the scary story goes, one lunch-time business meeting, our young fellow was serving as waiter to the top echelon of the area's movers & shakers, when he met—actually in the kitchen—an attractive young woman taking photos for a foodie magazine who, as it turned out, actually was the boss's daughter. They got to chatting, and seemed to hit it off. The fellow, feeling a bit nervous—she was attractive, and very receptive—felt the need to impress her. Not trusting his innate excellence or integrity, he began to brag, then to boast. He confessed to the young woman exactly how he was scamming his boss and—while scamming may be too harsh a word—he also told the attractive female that his boss and most of the station's TV-news watching public were ill-bred cretons, not worth the cost of the explosives to blow them sky high. The young girl—who on occasion was also known to call her father a creton, although not necessarily an ill-bred one—was sensitive about explosives. She had studied at Berkeley.

Two nights later, at a dinner for television news award winners, the top boss accepted a glass of pre-dinner wine from our ambitious fellow, then leaned over and spoke directly into our man's spray-tanned ear: "I know what you're trying to do, asshole. Now, go pick up your cosmetics bag at the station. Pack your apartment and get outta town. You're not only fired, you should never hope to work in television again, because you will not."

On campus, theater students shivered in fear. Some had begun to mirror a modified version of his campaign. Now his name was grass. Mud. Or Mudd. His career was *kaput*. His life in TV news, down the drain. For a period of time, the frightened students gathered each evening to search for deeper meaning, to discover the lesson, the message. What was the standard they should follow in their own lives? They were unsure, grasping for any idea, any practical philosophy to accept. What good is free will when the system is stacked against you? And isn't everything already predetermined, especially the accidents of life, the tragedies, a career in TV-News? This guy and what happened to him, what if a negative karma from a past life was changing, determining his present-time future?

Beyond the obvious, the most popular campus choice for meaning in all this was: Don't boast, don't "talk big," don't confide in the wrong people. Gina was sure there was a deeper lesson, like something about false pride. And maybe honesty. She decided to think about it.

Gina considered herself to be quite a realistic person. Before she set one foot in India or had settled into life in Vadodara, in the state of Gujarat, she had studied up and knew (but did not tell her parents) about the "Gujarat Pogrom," when a decade earlier murderous and majority Hindus ravaged, mass-raped, and mass-killed 790 unarmed Muslims. She had seen films and documentaries about the three-day killings and the following months of violence. Sadder but wiser, she generously declared *that* was then, *this* is now, and was surprised, on arrival, by the cosmopolitan look of Vadodara. She expected a dry countryside, endangered and starving people. So she felt pleased, and safer.

End of the school term where she helped the kids with English, day after day, Gina again turned her heart toward what she wanted most: To work with, to live with the tribes, the nomads of India, the *Bhils*. They told her to please wait just one more year, and she did so, being hopeful of living the simple life with the Bhils, away from what now seemed to be urbane Indian conglomeration.

That second year, they said, she was greatly needed to work in the nearby Labor and Delivery hospital which would be good training for when she was to be assigned to work with the tribes, the next year. She accepted and began to program her mind for labor and delivery.

Teaching English was behind her now. It had not been her cup of tea. She was not a natural teacher and never would be. She was disorganized and sloppy, she lost the kids' compositions, corrected test papers using the wrong answer key, and she was late turning in grades. But she loved those little imps, especially the six and seven-year olds. She loved the older kids as well, the honeybunch kids, and the quiet ones who would not speak, at first. Yes, she admitted, she had rowdy classes which made the administrators of the school shake their heads and mutter it must be some crazy American technique. She kept piles of stuff in her classroom, dried flowers and pieces of silk and a tiny junked engine, kid gifts.

Their affection for her roiled through her and stirred her own childhood emotions, and she ached to cling to her Indian children and never leave them. She was glad when weekends were over. Long holidays filled her with gloom. Might she have the same kids *next* year? Two years in a row? But she didn't ask. She kept her mouth zipped, had to. She knew she had not done much to help her students' English skills. Thank goodness the kids' previous teachers had prepared them so well. Gina's classes barely passed the standard test for English, but they easily yakked among themselves in soft casual American English. They had learned to like not just their special friends but everyone in the class—maybe in the world. They were sympathetic toward their parents who were once as young as they and the children were aware someday their parents would be elderly, needing their children just as today *they*, today's children, need their parents. In Gina Boswell's English class, they had learned, and taught each other, that kindness is king and r-e-s-p-e-c-t works. Most of the boys had a crush on their teacher and the girls dreamed of being just like her. Some kiddoes were always asking if they could go with her, walk her safely home. But that was not to be.

Walking trips home were, in truth, a bit of a problem. Usually teachers traveled in pairs, as many together as possible. Roaming groups of men were a well-known threat. A woman alone was an easy mark and to bring little children to the mix? Certainly not. Gina had been grabbed three different times while walking home alone, grabbed by men thinking it their right to paw and growl over women on a public street, pull them into an alley or around a pre-determined corner and rape them.

Such was the dilemma of India's young aimless men, angry men porked up on a perpetual diet of porn, but without possibility of a meet-up with a female. They were angry sex bombs ready to explode. And so many, but this was the unpleasant result of generations of families wanting baby boys, not girls, and when girls came anyhow, or were pictured in sonograms, they too often became "disappeared," were aborted and killed by their own families. Girls went missing because sons' wives provide the family with gifts and income, while daughters, if there were any, left with gifts and income intended for other families. Thus in certain segments of Indian society, some families were scraping the bottom of the Dispose-of-Girls-Here barrel, searching for daughters-in-law who might, in turn, give birth to beautiful Indian babies, the sons to be praised and well-fed, the daughters to go missing, be disappeared, or scrapped, like so much garbage, into the deadly bottom of the "Dispose-of-Girls-Here" bucket.

In a year's time, Gina had been approached six times by parents eager to discuss Gina's marriage with their sons. Less than a month ago, in fact, a group waved her down, one elderlyish man and two ladies in bright scarves and everyday jewelry on their wrists, necks, and foreheads. One lady thrust a pot of night flowering jasmine toward Gina, and as the gentleman explained: A young man of great worth, in their family, was most willing to meet her. He had right now a good job with the Gujarat telephone service. Only 30 years old. One of the ladies pulled out a file of some photographer's shots of Sonny smiling, standing, arms spread wide, next to a sports car, a ship, a tree.

Look, see. He exists. He *is* worthy. He was an exchange student in America, in Ohio. Gina was humbled. The heart-rending display by this family, for some reason, made her think of the song that says, "*...love the one you're with...if you can't be with the one you love, love the one you're with...*" She found tears ready to run down her cheeks. The group might rightly have assumed she had been won over. She had accepted the pot of night blooming jasmine but now Gina heard herself sadly telling them she was already married. She suspected the woman, dear mother-in-law, recognized the lie—because by some trick of nature mothers-in-law on any planet always recognize a lie—and would rip the plant from her at any moment. But the elderlish man spoke curtly and the family group, so close, yet so far, backed away, departing in an elderly trot, never seen again. Gina kept and tended her pot of night flowering jasmine which in India is known as the tree of sorrow.

As for the would-be rapists who brought neither plants nor their moms, *so far* Gina had been able to use her dance routine high kicks. One grabby fellow got kicked in the knee with the heel of a teacher's shoe. The other two received kicks more in the mid-body area. One suffered a twisted arm and the other would- be mugger or rapist got a knot on the head from a classroom clock Gina was carrying home to fix.

She thought somewhat longingly about the guns and knives available back home in Texas, but only texted Deidra to send her a few really loud rape whistles, some Mace spray thingamajigs—Gina would give her roommate, and some other girls, the means to save themselves—and, Gina sent a text to her mother, "Send me the miniature baseball bat." One of her daddy's friends at work brought back a couple of half—or quarter—size ball bats from a trip to Kentucky and a side-trip to the Museum and Bat Making Factory of the Louisville Slugger. "It's around the den somewhere," Gina wrote, and Deidra was so thrilled to help her daughter that rather quickly the package arrived and inside the daughter found beauty products, unasked for. "Hey! Momma bird, you did good," Gina said as tears ran down her face and she had to put her head down. Deidra had indeed also sent an assortment of whistles, a variety of aerosol containers: and

Mace, and the little bat, just so right for slugging would-be rapists any day of the week on the streets of Vedaddo in the state of Gujarat, in India.

At the end of Gina's suvivors's walk home each day, a boxy and modern apartment building welcomed her: Home at last, home at last, thank God almighty, home at last. She shared a simple two-room flat, and complete bathroom, with Debby. A chatty woman, Gina's roomie was a Christan nun from Botswana, Mma Debina. Mma was not a name. It was a title, like Sister or Miss or Ms—or Your Majesty. Gina asked to call her Debby, and Debby agreed. Twenty years older than Gina, Mma Debby appeared younger than her years, both in face and form. She was slender, and nice looking, almost glowing, as middle-aged celibate women often seem to be. She had a thousand questions about the churches in America, about the great distances between big cities. "They must be like kingdoms," she remarked.

Their first day together, Gina had to clandestinely find a quick way to research Botswana. Where the heck was it? But now, after a year together, Gina and Debby knew each other's country almost as well as they knew their own. On free days the two sometimes made their way to one or another shopping area where they found vivid shawls (they themselves had been advised to dress sedately) and block printed fabrics, many simply adorable, and Gina knew what she would be sending home next Christmas, or sooner: Slinky dresses for wearing under the shawls, and cutesy cotton creations, copies of which would soon be bundled off to WalMarts and Targets everywhere.

Gina and Debby saw so much to buy, wonderful fresh fruits and vegetables—innocent and bare, free of the power of curry and burn-your-brains-out peppers.

One remarkable shopping—but not buying—day, they walked past Peralia, with its "Ayurvedic roots," its supposed connection to the Himalayas. Debby and Gina looked at each other and shrugged. Gold leaf lettering on the pink glass front window promised, "As well as skin treatments and massages, Peralia offers reflexology, hydrotherapy, aromatherapy, and meditation." Debby said, "I know only meditation."

"Right on," Gina agreed, a bit confused, but in India she was often confused and at times felt forced to play along until things became clear. "We really should go to 'Meditations' more often. Take a cab over and back. After work, cab hop over to the church of Our Lady of the Forsaken, around five o'clock, what say?"

"Oh, I say that is the place for me. It certainly is."

Gina was stunned. Was her roommate just playing around, as the kids in Texas like to say, "Just playin' wid' you." Or was this a hint, a desperate hint? Could Gina help Debby? But in what way? "Why, Mma Debina, whatever do you mean?" Gina asked, protectively using her Southern USA accent, right there on the sidewalk in Vadodara. With no answer falling from Debby's lips, Gina dared to continue, speaking through closed teeth so that the accidental watcher might not think it was a cannabis deal in progress, "Listen, we both know Jesus, our Lord, that is, *Father, son, and Holy Spirit—the Blessed Trinity*—is never going to forsake you, no way, no how, never." She repeated, "Father, son, and Holy Spirit, *three persons*, Debby, one God," because if Gina Boswell was anything, she was a Trinitarian, a Trinitarian Catholic. She recognized, loved and was forever mentally alert to the idea of the three-personed God, an idea most Christians support but don't think much about.

Faith and a growing link to the Trinity may have been why Gina lived her life with such practical disregard for doubt. She meant what she said to Debby. And while Debby-Debina seemed near tears and still offered no answer, Gina, Miss Mid-Texas 2013, knew exactly what to do. "Guess what," she announced, "let's go have a facial. Ever have a facial? No? Don't worry, Ok, Mma Debina? Let us go because I am paying. My mother sent me some money." It wasn't literally true but the boast made Miss Mid-Texas feel less guilty about leaving Deidra at home alone. With just Gina's dad who isn't much company for any delicate lonely birdie.

As it turned out, the facial they decided to try was "Platinum" which included an after-application of cosmetics, *fond de teint crème doux*, eye-liner, lashes, blush, lip-liner, the works. So Gina paid, smiling to her own greedy soul; she had beaucoup money. Money, money, money. Mma Debby, the Boswanaian nun, a woman in her mid-forties, left Peralia smiling because for the first time perhaps in her life she was feeling simply but strangely beautiful.

Debby claimed to have felt excitement when President Obama first won the American election. She called him cousin and wanted to like him, but could not. She especially had a hard time trying to like him after she saw clips of one of the White House Correspondents' Dinners. "The man is insane," she told Gina who lamely answered, "All that was a joke, Debby," and Debby answered, "Yes, nobody likes him, even his wife." So Gina told her, "The next election is coming. He's done. His goose is cooked."

"What? Oh, I see. He has done something of scandal?" Mma asked and Gina said, "Something of scandal?—How would we ever really know?—and tried to explain that a US president can only serve two four-year terms. "Obama has had two terms. He must go away."

Debby was assigned to the school again for another year. She took her assignment as neither here nor there. She shrugged stoically. Her life was not her own.

"*Detachment*, yay, that's just *the* best thing, the *only* way to live," Gina babbled, but with admiration. She was still fighting with herself about having to face *another* damn year away from the Bhils, the Catholic tribe in danger of being swallowed up by cheerful anti-Catholic Protestants or chewed into bloody pieces by Hindus demanding their ouster, the death of all Christians. Deb told her that God had been holding onto the Bhiels, keeping them Catholic for hundreds of years, maybe longer. "They can wait one year for your arrival, can't they, Sugar?" And Gina wondered if Deb was making fun of her? And what was with that weird accent, *Sugar*?

Labor and Delivery. Daily Gina teetered on and over the line between jumping up and down to cheer the sweet triumph of a completed and happy birth for Baby A or falling to the floor in tears at the sad arrival of Baby B, alive and lively in the womb, but who died during the birth struggle. Why? What disparity causes this heartbreak? Gina had promised herself that, while she would do her best for all the little ones she was responsible for, she would give extra cuddles to Babies C, little Indian *girls*. She would watch out for them, and ply their parents with *blah blah & la la* stories about how American families go *gaga* over their little girls. She would knock herself out trying to persuade the baby girls' parents that the future is thriving and alive with opportunities, scholarships, and advanced college and university degrees for young women worldwide, but that especially rural, village and country-dwelling women in India will, in 15 years, discover that banks—indeed, indeed, the places where money is kept—will be interested in giving low interest loans, yes, *in India* to both rural and downtown/uptown young women. Heck, those banking people are even going out to look for women and girls who want to start small businesses, or who are artists or musicians, or *storytellers:* The banks in India—as in America—will want to connect storytellers with theaters, and acting classes, and even with the amazing script-writing departments of Bollywood.

She would tell them that back home, all across America, families joke that it costs them less to see their girl get a college education than to give her a big wedding because an educated daughter can easily pay for her own wedding. In fact, back home in the USA, all up and down and across America, the *dads* are especially proud when their girls end up making as much money as their fathers. In America— just as in India—it seems the the youngest generation is, more and more, the one to "be there" for their parents as they age. And isn't it always, of all the kids, the daughters who have the biggest hearts, ready to see to the care of Mom and Daddy, especially when those *girls,* and future leaders of the nation, are also knocking down the big bucks? You know, "top dollar," millions and billions of rupees.

Gina had set aside several evenings before Labor and Delivery got started for the year and, with Debby's help, had made hundreds of pink "baby girl" souvenirs. When time came for mom, and maybe pop, to leave the hospital with their adorable daughter, Gina would show up, smiling ear to ear, bragging on the baby and giving the parents a little nothing, just a very small pink cloud of nothingness to help them remember the birth of this important girl. Gina didn't care if she overdid it. She figured she had a captive audience and so why not? She hoped her words would be seeds planted deep within the hearts and minds of India's girls' parents.

And then, there is Baby D. For reasons beyond Gina's ability to understand, the cruelest and most tragic loss of all, was when perfectly beautiful babies—or challenged ones—born alive to everyone's appreciation, simply gave up and died within hours. Why did so many Indian babies die? How can a country go about its business when for every 1,000 births, *thirty-seven* newborns die? This was a 2014 statistic, fresh off the presses.

One evening, Gina made a chart, with Debby's help, a design to help them both memorize other 2014 numbers on the subject of infant mortality. Gina's number chart was in no particular order, other than to make it easy for her to remember the stats and, in a comfortable manner, spiel off the correct numbers to support her refusal to admit any normality in thirty-seven deaths per one thousand deliveries in India. She hoped her pocket-packet of information would be like passing the baton to someone, the fresh runner, who could carry it to the finish line.

Herewith is Mma Debby and Gina's cleaned-up and ultimately sorted information, or some of it, the highlights: India had 37 infant deaths in every 1,000 births. Botswana—sorry, Mma Debina—had 34.5 infant deaths in every 1,000 births. Indonesia had 24.3 deaths in 1,000 births. Brazil: 14.6 deaths in 1,000 births. Turkey: 11.1 deaths in 1,000 births. The Czeck Republic: 8.4 deaths in 1,000 births. The United States: 5.9 deaths in 1,000 births.

She understood. So many people, so many deaths. Workers get home from a long day, tired, half-angry. They don't want to be preached at about dead kids—what can *anyone* do about it—let's just make the most of the night. Forget all the sadness. Gina steeled herself against emotional involvement with her tiny babies, but she raged inwardly, and grieved each infant's death. In this far-away India, a place unknown and unattached to her, it was in this place where Gina Marie learned true sorrow, where she ached at the sight of coming death, burned at the chilling touch of each dear and dying babe. But, no anger, no tears, she took the mothers to her heart. Whatever comes next, Gina hoped her mothers in India would remember not the pain of birth, pain that was supposed to be soon forgotten—but, prove it, please. Gina, still virginal, didn't believe it, but while birth may be forgotten. Death is not. No, she hoped each mother, whatever happened to her in the days and years to come, would remember that some hospital person was holding her hand and softly singing "...*I am weak, but thou art strong... Jesus keep me from all wrong*," sort of a Patsy Cline birth chant in Gujarat, in the steamy warm forests of Vadodara, on the banks of the Vishwamitri river, where babies were born and too many babies died. "... *Thou art strong...*"

Gina's research taught her that there are perhaps up to 4 million Bhils, called gypsies by some, nomads, or indigenous peoples by others, who live in one place or in many places— within the Gujarat area. She threw her Deidra hands up and muttered in a San Mateo pout, "Good grief! How can they not know *where* the hell the people are. Too bad they don't wear signs, saying 'Over here, look at me, I'm a Bhils and I will happily identify myself for you.'" Gina considered her library print-out again: "Bhils, said to be the rather populous remnant of some historic Catholic tribal unit...Bhils are also said to be in such an advanced condition that they allow themselves to mix well with the outside culture and are turned on, rather than off, by the use of technology..."

"They sound *Indian* to me," Gina sulked. "But where are they?" she asked, as her third year reared its head and began to wiggle its ears. She was beginning to accept the idea that, like Leprechauns and fairies, the Bhils exist only on holidays or on back roads deep into forests so green they are deep blind black. And no person has probably ever even seen them.

The administrators of Gina's missionary work hinted that if she stayed for a fourth year, she might just get to work one-on-one with the families of the Bhils. As it is, they told her, Gina had probably already visited *téte-à-téte* with any number of Bhils, not so much at the school, no, no, but more than likely in Labor and Delivery, yes, yes. Gina was tempted to ask for names, dates, and why not photos of a new Bhils infant coming out of Delivery? And if there had been Bhils in-and-out of the hospital, wouldn't it be nice if the L & D personnel were to visit those families again? But she let it go.

The first fact, and reason, she let it go was that she was tired. The second fact was that *they* wanted her back in Labor and Delivery, not the other way around, and Gina, not our original San Mateo Gina, but still Gina, was not so tired that she'd completely abandon a situation where she had the upper hand. Fact three was that Gina was hooked on India's babies. She was infatuated with the nation's infant babies. She was just as in love with those babies as if she had found them along the garden path, each one tied up in bright ribbons and sitting in a basket of daisies. The number four fact she didn't still ask to be relieved of maternity duty was because—possibly the real fantasy number one—a certain young obstetrician seemingly had taken a fancy to her. And why not stay in L & D, make time with the ever-flowing stream of babies, and just see what happens with the doc, and at the same time cause the administrators to feel guilty about keeping her from the Bhis, so guilty she might get to go home early. When she realized her thinking and plotting was as convoluted and dishonest as the original Gina had been in her worst of moments in early Texas, she sat down, shook her head, and wept herself asleep.

Debby had gone or had been sent back early to Botswana at the start of her third year. Gina was relocated to a flat nearer the hospital, and her second roomie was a Dutch woman most recently from Mumbai. Gina already missed Mma Debina more than she thought possible. Fretting over how she would ever see her again, Gina grumbled, sure, airplanes fly up, up, up but so did the price of tickets go up, up, up. Even more, she brooded over why Debby left so quickly and didn't fess up, never told her why. That hurt. Since the day of their platinum facials, Gina had worried that she, her worldliness, her Americaness, might have caused Debby some sort of discontent.

Well into year three, Gina felt herself bumbling along. On one hand, needing rather desperately to go home, she was, on the other hand, willing, willy-nilly, to live on in-country until, she guessed, they bodily threw her out. That was a joke. In truth, India seemed intent on claiming her, much more than she would want to claim India. Romantic matters remained in a stalemate since the doctor seemed to be more interested in peek-a-boo games, now you see me all charming and polished, then you see me not at all. Indeed, Gina was in a rut and may have remained so except for "the great trouble."

After years of discussion and debate, India was re-structuring its adoption laws so that applicants were no longer required to be heterosexual married couples. It was a bow to the gay and lesbian lifestyle. But besides allowing gay and lesbian people to adopt, the proposed change in the process also opened the doors for single, older, and the disabled who wanted to raise a child to file paperwork to adopt. The re-structuring was an idea refused by traditional Catholicism in India at that time which was early days for Francis, real name Jorge Bergoglio, the new pope in Rome. Few could have predicted the degree of division and the amount of disappointment and angst Catholics worldwide would feel when this man from Argentina revealed his "Who-am-I-to-judge dismissiveness of church traditions especially in matters of marriage and "gender choice."

Gina, rarely infected by what other people thought workable, nevertheless was soaking in a certain pool of thought that suggested she, at age 23, coming up to 24, had a biological clock ticking, ticking, ticking her presumed fertility into timeless nothingness. There was to be no respite for Gina. And not much hope either, she thought. Still very pretty, if not quite beautiful after more than three years of missionary work, she once again rode a fast train into her grade school moodiness. It began to possess and oppress her. With no fiancé waiting at home, no male acquaintance hiding in India's mangrove bushes, Gina took it that she was facing a childless future. As a single woman, would her faith in the precepts and doctrines of Catholicism prevent *her* from adopting? If so, she was doomed. To live her faith—in India—she could be doomed never to be a mother. She began to speak out.

"To speak out" in India was quite unlike having a stateside spitting screaming contest with your parents or not answering the phone out of spite or throwing a rinky-dink fit to get what you want. She knew she absolutely had to grow up, and she made a decision. She would support India's new adoption policy. She would speak, write, call, attend protests, go to jail, all in favor of adoption so that single women could become single mothers.

Before you can actually say Bollywood, the American woman from Texas, the *Catholic* American woman named Gina Boswell, was all over India's news, calling down the church for its cruel-hearted bigotry and prejudice against the homosexual community as well as offending single, older and handicapped men and women everywhere. Almost overnight she became the gay group's babydoll and the lesbian clique's tricycle. She was the Catholic Church's Benedict Arnold, her very own Judas Iscariot. *But, but, but*—Gina was left with her index finger in the air, trying to say, "Wait, wait, guys, y'all misunderstand. What I meant to say..."

Ah, yes. We understand, Gina. Like countless souls before, and after, the inestimable Boswell woman had chosen fear, self-interest, and the precarious error of speaking out on a hot-button issue without considering the safe resting zone known as moral ground. Or common sense. Sadly, slip-sliding self-interest, even for the sweetest of reasons, does not outweigh moral-interests. May a person vote for an appealing candidate, who speaks one's lingo on some issues, and, more importantly, promises benefits for you and your crew—say he or she vows to forgive all student loans—but the candidate also stands for issues that are morally repugnant? Consider: Gina needed help. She had chosen wrongly. To be the person she claimed to be, aspired to be, she needed to back away from her publicly and widely known choice. But how?

The easy way out of her dilemma would be simply to leave the country. She no longer had a job or a sponsor, talk about *loss of perks*, but at the same time—the devil on overload— producers were calling, hinting at offers for parts in films. She was wanted for interviews. People were anxious to see her. She looked good, was attractive, had theater experience, could sing and dance. What might these Bollywood agents mean in her life? Was it recompense for her present disgrace? It wasn't tribes, but Bollywood was still something mighty special.

The time difference between Vadodara, Gujarat and San Mateo, Texas was ten hours and thirty minutes, for some reason, with Vadodara coming in ahead. Gina set the alarm on her cell phone for two-thirty AM, a Monday. She lay on her cot, awake all night, fortunately, because the alarm failed to work. Her contact, her erstwhile advisor, her life line, was in for one giant surprise.

Lynsey Gerardi asked her, "Do you have your passport in hand, travel documents and a ticket back to Texas?"

"I do, and I have a ticket, but just to New York."

The voice from Mid-Texas asked, "Gina. Are you involved with a man, someone you love in India?"

Gina felt the way she did that day back at school, back at work at Jitterbug, after she had shaved half her hair off. Tears rolled down her face. "Miss Lynsey, I love every man, woman, and child, in India, but no, ma'am, no one in particular, no one to mention, no, it's just me, selfish old know-it-all Gina."

"Ok, then," Lynsey said, and Gina felt a sparkle, a *Sparkle-a-Plenty*, in her oldest friend's voice. "I'll have Preston arrange a ticket for *one, uno,* from New York to Austin. Since we don't need a ticket for *him*. Now. Call your parents and ask them to pick you up at the Austin airport. Since you'll be on your lonesome."

For the first time in her life, Gina felt something, a warm flame glowing somewhere in her heart, her mind. "I want that, more of *that*, that kind of Lynsey Gerardi love and understanding," she said aloud, laughing, because even in surrender there is still selfishness, the call for self-preservation. After the way Miss Lynsey just accepted and *helped* her, Gina knew she would survive and she decided she would pay it back, or as kids in America were saying, "pay it *forward*." In less than a week, she was back in San Mateo. In less than a month she had a job at the Roeller County Children's Shelter and in six more months she had found a child, a little girl, living temporarily at the shelter where she worked. The child didn't need a single mother. She needed a kidney. They were a match. In six weeks Gina had given away a kidney, a goodly section of her pride and most of her arrogance. A year ago she invited her parents to drive to New Orleans with her and she paid but they insisted on paying her back. A year or two before that, she met Casey J. Greene, an engineer, a fellow who worked his way through grad school by substitute teaching at the high school Gina had attended. It was he, a substitute teacher working his way gradually through college, *his* voice that broke up the pack of kids taunting her that Monday after she'd had half her hair shaved off. He now had a PhD and was back in San Mateo, doing research at a government lab in North Roeller. It was he who convinced Gina to finish her studies, but not in theatre. Under Casey's influence, she began classes to become a medical technician, and was working full-time, for now, at All Saints Methodist Hospital.

She and Casey had celebrated their marriage in a beautiful but simple wedding—the bride wore a red silk saree with tons of bling and a jade ring tied to a gray velvet ribbon around her neck. Casey wore a tux and cowboy boots. And on Wednesday, March 25th, it was Gina who had been chosen to go to the drive-through because she, being an expectant mother—expecting in about a week or so—could park upfront, close to the hospital's only open entrance, all others being closed because of COVID. She and a co-worker, Tiffany Barr, had driven to Crunchy Chicken's to pick up early dinners/late lunches for six starving med-techs at the hospital. Back in All Saints parking lot, Gina had just managed to find a spot in the Stork's special row for expectant mothers and was getting herself out of the car when she felt amniorrhexis, a warm flash over her hips and legs. "I think I've just peed on myself," she whispered.

"Your water's broke, silly," Tiffany, who has two young children, informed her. Gina, out of her mind with sudden excitement, and Tiffany began wildly gathering the paper sacks and styrofoam containers. "Look," Tiffany said, "somebody is getting a chopper ride. Must be big."

The two women started for the entrance. "I'm all wet," Gina complained. Walking stiffy, appalled at herself, still dripping, she whined, "What am I gonna *do?*"

"Well, you're *not* going back to the lab," Tiffany told her. "I'm going to get you a wheelchair. Wait here. Let's put these chickens on this car, right over there. *Ooo.* A Mercedes. Oh, well."

Gina bent, felt a tightening at her waist. "Tiff," she screamed, "in this damn car, that laptop! I know who owns it, and this isn't her car!"

Leaning on the Mercedes, Gina pulled at the door. It opened. Reaching in, she tugged at the laptop. "Let *me*," Tiffany insisted and asked, "Can we just take it?"

"Look on the bottom," Gina yelled and Tiffany squinted and yelled back, "Says Lynsey Gerdoff."

"We're takin' it," Gina bellowed. "You carry the chickens, I've got the lap—" and a slow and strange pain hit her, knocking her breath out.

Together they staggered toward the entrance, making it from car to car, Gina clutching the laptop, Tiffany, spilling fried chicken pieces on the sidewalk and yelling at the top of her lungs, "Labor and Delivery! Somebody get a wheelchair. Her water's broke! *Help.* Get somebody from Labor and Delivery! Labor and Delivery!"

"'Labor and Delivery," Gina said, panting, "I like that."

Chapter seven ~ the Trip

"...fountains mingle with the river"

Love's Philosphy

-Percy Bysshe Shelley

Staying within the standard 70 mph speed limit on Interstate 35 South, the butter blonde behind the wheel could not believe her good fortune. She had not only managed to meet Preston Gerardi. Right now, at this exact moment, she had him. He was a passenger in her Chevy Equinox. He could neither escape nor fail to answer her questions, and if he did, she'd just dump him off on the side of the highway. For three seconds, she readied herself to say that, tell him he is her prisoner. But feminine instinct and smarts prevailed. After all, she had offered to drive him from San Mateo to the trauma hospital at SAMMC, San Antonio Military Medical Center. The fastest way to the trauma ER was a straight shot to the North East side of San Antonio. Supposedly forty-eight minutes by car, twenty-four by air. If the guy's calculations were correct, she, the blonde driver, estimated that Lynsey Gerardi, Preston's 87-year-old mother, would be leaving San Mateo aboard a medevac helicopter in about fourteen minutes.

The blonde behind the wheel had to work fast. She glanced at Preston Gerardi. Flashing a sideways smile, she told him, "Somebody said your mom keeps a journal. Has for many years." When he didn't answer with the speed that she expected, she repeated herself, shortening, simplifying her question: *"I've heard your mother keeps a journal."*

"Does she?" Preston asked, momentarily studying her, his driver, wondering if it were possible, in nature, for an adult woman, over thirty, probably, to have hair the color of butter. He was wondering how, in God's name, he came to be sitting next to a real, live, seriously beautiful woman. He was concerned and upset; did he let this happen?

His question-answer threw her for a loop. Cinnah Shelton of Cal-Tex News & Mysteries, Inc., wasn't used to people, men especially, making her feel awkward. Or stupid. She shot him what she considered to be a questioning look. It was supposed to say, why would you be rude to me when I am so adorable, and much smarter than you.

He laughed because he didn't know what else to do, and she said in a semi-pout, "Journalling is a great way to get in touch with your feelings. You should try it."

Oh, hell. Now he had hacked her off. Preston was not a cruel man. He was not even easily annoyed. Long ago he had learned to fend off manipulative, attractive, willing women. Usually he would close the gates and move to his interior. "Yes," he said in a tired voice, "she has been keeping a diary or a journal since she was 13 years old, and I have been surreptitiously reading them, every single page, since I was about ten years old. All of us kids read her journals. My sister still does, when she's here. It gets to your mind. The way she thinks."

The woman gasped. Maybe the guy wasn't such a stuffed shirt after all. "Y'all read your mother's journals? For real?"

"Yeah, she thinks it's fairies or something. Calls us *her readers*. She used to set traps, trying to catch us, someone." *Her readers.*

Preston almost gave into tears, but he focused on his annoyance: This little lady should not have gone for the jugular. He wasn't in mood for picky-ass questions.

"And," Cinnah asked, "are they good?"

"What? Her journals?" Preston pulled himself together. Ok, girlie. "As a record of time and events, they are stupendous. As literature, they are gibberish, wig wag, drive ya crazy," he said, turning for a closer look at her and she whispered to the man, the bad boy at her side, "Shame on you. I bet they are sweet."

"You don't know my mother," Preston said. He knew he should guard his eyes. Pushy, he reminded himself. The way this gal had elbowed her way into his conversation with Fausto had bugged him. Still bugged him. Preston had planned to have the sheriff drive him to San Antonio in his official county sheriff's vehicle. For one thing, getting onto the military post was going to be hell. He seldom mentioned it, but the military was his second thing. "I could have been a Marine colonel," he sometimes smiled and said to himself. Now he said to the blonde, "Just ask me, I'll tell you whatever you want to know. Or part of it." Preston was fond of being in charge. "Ask Preston" had become a faint mantra or night time lullaby all around Roeller County. Little echoes of "Ask Preston" drifted through city offices and emergency services. Preston was someone who'd know how to talk down suicidal riverbridge jumpers, settle various confrontations, tell you where you can get your hands on real money real quick. He was a nerd, a geek; he knew how to put a bandaid on so it will stay the rest of the week. Or fix your wifi. He was available to everyone, belonged to no one. He liked it that way.

But he had no way to smooze the military. They didn't know him, and since 9-11, the military had gone wacko nuts. With coronavirus, they were going to be full-on bas-astards about visitors getting on post. Preston figured the Roeller County Sheriff, lights flashing, would have gotten him wherever he wanted to be: In charge.

But then here came Miz Nosey-Posey. What's her name? Shana? Well, she just had to blurt out that the sheriff couldn't leave the county in the middle of an investigation into Mrs. Gerardi's attack and that she, herself, could drive Mr. Gerardi to San Antonio. And get him to talk. Not bloody likely. Preston ground his jaws together. People, women usually, had been trying for over fifty years to find the key to unlock his taciturnity. Who does this one think she is, Erin Andrews? Maria Bartiromo? *Ba-Ba* Walters?

"You don't talk much," Cinnah observed.

Preston didn't answer. He had begun making plans because Faus Dellheim had indeed promised to phone ahead, to warn the military mucky-mucks at the gate, at the hospital, that he, Preston Gerardi, surviving son of Lynsey Gerardi— who would soon to be arriving via Air Life chopper—would be on post at about the same time to see about his mother's wellbeing, so cut him some slack. Faus had offered to send a car down, when the next shift changed, to pick him up. That had suited Preston perfectly because he planned ASAP to dump Miss American journalist—what did she do, write a blog? He would tell her the deputy would drive him back. Bye-bye. *Raus mit.* Preston remembered a few words from his high school German, words he seldom used when he was stationed there: *Off you go,* get up, be gone. *Raus.* He'd get a ride, no problem.

No, Preston did not drive. He did not drive *himself.* He himself did not drive. In *Texas?* How unusual. Must be something wrong with him. People who kept track of strange things reckoned he was AA and had been caught drunk driving too many times or he had macular degeneration. To Preston, not having to drive, being free to do something, anything, when trapped in a car, a bus, a train, a boat or plane, or on an enforced shopping trip with a female, was the highest luxury, a virtue, next only to minding your own damn business. He was rather proud of not driving. Besides, he liked having a driver. He had a semi-regular driver, old Jimmy Pitman, who was fifteen years younger than Preston, but he was retired, retired military. You retire, you die. *Damn!* Why hadn't he thought to call Jimmy? *Crap.*

Whatever. Dump the woman. Hire *Uber.* Or call Jimmy, what could be easier?

As if she were reading his mind, Blondie asked, "You don't like to drive?"

"Look," he explained to her, "I appreciate you taking time to get me to San Antonio. I really do. Yes, I'm not much of a talker. No, I don't like to drive. I have a license. And insurance. Having insurance in Roeller County is a high class thing, you know? I even own a car. Hit my car, we're good to go. You're in big hands. Now, I accepted your offer, knowing full well that you have questions, that you've been waiting, lying in the grass, munching away, so to speak, because you want to get the story—the thing is, there is no story. And who are these people who want to know? I guess somebody somewhere is paying you to ask me about my mother, my habits, my business. I wouldn't exactly call it an even exchange, but Ok, just do it. Shoot. Ask what you want to know."

"It doesn't have to be like this," she said, ever so softly.

"We agree. Hey. 'I don't need things to be easy, I need things to be worth it.' Lil Wayne. *Really*. He said that. Amuses the hell outta me."

"Ok," she said.

"That's why we are having an early spring. *Lil Wayne*, little rain? See?"

"Oh, Ok," she said. "I get it."

"I doubt that, but, you see, while you have my gratitude for the ride, may I remind you that earlier today my ancient mother was attacked at the home we share. I was not there. But yes, at 63, I still live with my mother. Why? Because neither of us could ever convince the other to move out, and no, I have never been married. No, I am not gay. Yes, I will tell you that I am Roman Catholic, struggling, but a classic Catholic. Short of them shooting me, I remain Catholic. I like it. I can tell you my youngest sister has had lung cancer, and my other sister, the nice one, in Scotland, is getting a divorce, and no, all my income does not come from Jitterbug. We diversified ages ago. I have one nephew. Kid lives in Spain—and unhappily, I think, my *nice* sister is actually in Spain right now—and it seems he, my sister's eight-year-old grandson, will inherit every dang thing. Until then, thank God, I am into technology, have been all my life. I'm working to develop my innate, low-level, talent for photography. Pictures, color. *Clic-clic*. Seeing things my way, freezing them for eternity. And, in the time I have left, after avoiding certain people's questions, I do martial arts.

Combat, self-defence, Taekwondo, karate, kickboxing. Krav Maga. Like *that*." He winked at her.

"Impressive," she said.

"Thank you, and now if you don't mind, I will sleep and relax my mind the rest of the way to the *ci-ty*."

Preston was a big guy trying to get comfy in a small seat. No matter. He closed his eyes, muttered a quick and indifferent prayer for Lynsey Gerardi's general well-being, and allowed his memory to travel once again to some summer day, long ago, a well-worn day that likely never happened, when he and Catherine Lemke—*surprise, surprise*—were in this very same area, in the nearby river, floating placidly down the clear clean Guadalupe River, bubbling along together, each encircled by the innertube of a giant truck. It came to be called tubing. A Mid-Texas present day tradition: Tubing down the Guadalup,' dropping the *e*. You could stretch your head back, then, at that time, and feel the sunlight, the splash of water droplets on your face, and hear Catherine nearby wondrously singing "Hotel California." Open your eyes, it is Eden, green and cool, floating pure, no tractors, no trailers, no pick-up trucks. No drunk idiots. Just undisturbed beauty, it was days like that convinced those tough old settlers from Germany, Ireland, Turkey, New Orleans, Baltimore and Bohemia that they could indeed stay one more year, or ten, or sixty, in this wild land, this *Texas*. Most immigrants soon enough learned to respect the Texas sun, never work naked, even in the shade, stay only brief hours in direct sunlight, even covered up. Stay dressed, you will be cooler.

Preston, the would-be old cowboy, high-school educated mama's boy, professional grump, solitary soldier, committed isolate, was once again 17 or maybe 18, an age when he worked six days a week in his family's business. Managing the business, he said.

Back then, at times, girls—*chicas*—pressed him for the facts, "Not in college? Where exactly do you work?"

"At Jitterbug's."

"What do you do there?"

"I dance," he'd say and they'd scowl and move away.

Being at home in those days, when Preston was slogging his way through high school, was identical to being at work; the only difference was that *work* was not a museum, a cathedral, dedicated to two deceased brothers and filled with crying teenage sisters.

On summer Sundays then, after sitting through Mass together with his mother and sisters, avoiding the stares, the timid smiles of sympathy, he would escape into his Texan mode, and, like as not, find himself floating down the river's clear shallow water, tubing on the *Guada-loop*. Free of the constant sorrow, and holding an arm out, he could just barely reach Catherine's fingers. She had the sweetest face, pretty even with wet stringy hair. She was almost a double for Valerie Bertinelli. And her voice, it was a gift. She didn't have the foggiest idea what Hotel California was about. If he had told her, she might have said, "Oh, well, it sounds like an opium den."

"Catherine," Preston said to the fleeting image of young Cate Lemke, "where are you today? Be well. Stay home, wherever home may be."

Preston sat up and reached for his cell phone. What are the chances? She might be on FaceBook. Cinnah watched him research his cell and assumed it was business or a hospital question. It didn't take long. Just a few minutes before he realized this was the wrong time and place. He shrugged, and gave his driver a half-grin. What was her name? Shana?

She cleared her throat and said, "My mother is in a nursing home. She's only 68, but she has Alzheimer's." Preston whistled in the air, said he was sorry to hear that. Cinnah was trying to be professional, distant. "She has to be watched *all* the time. I tell you, I am worried sick with this coronavirus. I wish we had something like Jitterbug in Belwin. I'd bring her home in a heartbeat."

"Belwin, in what county did you say?" Preston asked. "By the way, what is your name, how do you say it?'

"Belwin, in Dell County. And my mother says my name is C-I-N-N-A-H. *Cinnah*. The way she always said it, it sounds like sinner. *Sinnah*. Just don't try to turn it into cinnamon buns."

"Who me? No, never, but that's interesting. Where did she come up with Cinnah?"

"Now you're interviewing me."

"Yeah, I like it. Are you married? Divorced?"

"Divorced. Four years. And annulled. Don't ask, and don't call it a Catholic divorce. It's much more than that."

Preston chuckled. "Damn right. *Much* more. I know people who call an anullment 'the eighth sacrament.'"

"That's a bit crude," she grinned, "but I like it."

Preston sat up tall, did a double take. "Are you really serious about bringing your mother home"—Cinnah cut in, "I certainly am! *Why?*"—"Well," Preston continued, "it just so happens—you are not going to believe this—we do have an agency in Dell County. For about a year now."

"Really?" Cinnah was confused—and he cut in, "Except it's not called Jitterbug. It's called Bergeron's Agency. Bergeron is my mother's maiden name. And since—"

Cinnah began to backtrack. "It's pretty expensive?"

"Well, you get what you pay for, much as suits you. She's 68? It may not be as costly as you think, considering what you're being charged for the nursing home. You'd bring her to your house? At least during *corona*? And you live, perhaps, alone? Without help?"

"With my dad and my eight-year-old son, Kevin. *Kev.*" And Preston announced, almost shouting, "That's great, you have a boy. I always wanted me a boy."

Cinnah's ears went on alert, for what, she wasn't sure, but she casually told him, "I was 40 when he was born."

He nodded approvingly, "Well then, you're nearly 50."

"Just turned forty-eight," she said.

"Tell you what," he said, "you think it over. I can have somebody send—*naw*, I'll do it myself. You may be surprised. I'll get you some information. I think it'll work,"

"I'd be surprised if you couldn't sell angels wings."

"Do a lot of people try to sell you wings?" He said it like wangs. *Wangs.*

She laughed. "No, I meant *you* could sell *wings* to angels, refrigerators to icemen? It was a compliment, understand? *Sheee.* A bit touchy, are we?"

"No, you just have me totally confused. Do *you* understand?"

"I think so," she said and reached over and took his hand. Breathless at her own audacity, she almost fainted when he continued to not only hold her hand but to cling to it. She told him what she usually told her eight-year-old when she didn't know what was going on, "It'll be alright. Don't worry." And then she added, "I will stay with you, when we get to the hospital, Ok?"

Preston, not normally a man who needs to be concerned over duplicity since he simply avoided situations where either untruths or utter truthfulness were necessary, was asking himself if it was necessary to mention his original plan about dumping her. Instead, he decided to warn her of the futility of it all. "You know, thanks to COVID, and the military being a buncha tightasses, they may not even allow me to see her. Might not even let us in the building. Hell, we may not even be allowed through the gate."

"Oh, *that's* why you wanted the sheriff to drive you—you wanted flashing lights to get you on the post, and I poked my nose in your business. Sorry, now you're stuck with me."

Preston Gerardi could not speak. His mind was firing off in all directions. He wanted to make a snarky comment about the color of her hair. To test *her.* Force her to reject him, to piss her off. Instead, he pulled her hand to his lips and kissed her college ring.

She laughed. "That's Ok, I'll be the pope." She pulled their hands to her and made a blessing, akin to the sign of the cross. "I bless you. And I'll stay with you, wait outside, whatever it takes. We'll just do whatever they say. Whatever it takes to see about your mom."

"Too bad we can't stop to get something to eat. COVID means everything, except drive-through, is closed. Bars, closed. Restaurants, closed. We need to get to know each other, a little better, before—"

"*Before* what?" she asked.

"Before we send out the announcements, shouldn't we spend time together? We could go to a hotel—"

She grabbed her hand away from him and wiped it off. "I think I know you already, completely, and too well!" She shivered, in disgust, in revulsion. They sat, no one speaking until Cinnah couldn't endure it. Since she was already more than halfway to the hospital, she waved the flag of truce, "Ok, simply out of respect for your mother who is at the trauma hospital, seriously ill, I am going to just ignore you and make sure *she* gets taken care of, that *she* knows someone was there for her. Now be quiet, and let me hear my GPS. Do not speak. You really are better when you don't talk. So, don't say two words to me. Just call the sheriff and tell him, so that he knows I will be driving back to San Mateo tonight, with you or without you. Understand?"

"I'm sorry, I'm sorry. Cinnah. I should not have said that word, hotel, motel, to you. I was just testing you. Teasing. Trying to make you—but we can surely do what you say, what you will do, which—I promise you—is vastly more than I deserve and a great deal more than I dared hope for."

They drove in silence, though afternoon traffic began to slow their journey. Preston made a call on his cell and spoke tersely with someone in the sheriff's office, canceling the ride home, thanking the person, asking him or her to tell the sheriff his mother would so much appreciate the consideration.

"Does this mean I can't bring my mother home?" Cinnah asked.

"Absolutely not, absolutely not. No, no. I believe you will be surprised and pleased. We can do that first thing in the morning. We'll get that rolling first thing. In the morning."

Again checking his phone, he said, "Because of all that's happened, I, you know, have calls to make. You have permission to listen. In fact, I'd love it if you'd just make the calls for me." He threw his hands up, "Kidding, kidding," he said and she said, "No, you're not."

"I gotta call Sarah." Preston got set to call someone—this Sarah person—and Cinnah felt annoyed. Who is this Sarah? She fumed, uncomfortable, but why? She didn't care.

"*Yoli?* How-are-you? Yes, dear, thank you, thank you. I am going to the hospital right now. *Por favor?* Don't know what Squad Two has in the morning? Yeah, about nine. I'll be there or y'all come on in. Ok, see you then."

He didn't really want to make these damn calls in front of *her*, but what choice did he have?

"Hello, Stevie. Yes sir, thank you, very kind. It was, it was. You know, I am going to the hospital right now. Well, one thing I know, we're going to need your services. Yeah, place was pretty wrecked. Thanks, appreciate it, Buddy. Nine sounds great. Be lookin' at you."

Preston asked Cinnah, "Did you have lunch?" She nodded. He made another call. "Max. God bless you, man. Yes sir, quite a shock. I'm Ok. Oh, right now, you know the drill, hospital, hospital, but they haven't told us anything yet. The thing is, that damn front door has got to have major repairs, be replaced. Sarah's gonna call you, Ok. About nine? Don't know. Blue, red. Ask Sarah. Yep, she is. Gottcha, Buddy. God bless. See ya then."

He stared at Cinnah for a long minute. "I think so, we can get your mother set up—is Monday too soon? Be thinking about how we're going to pull this off. It's almost end of the month, if you're month-to-month. We'll see. I need to call this guy I never met. Hang on for a bit."

The sheriff had given him a card, and Preston was searching himself for it. "Here's the damn name." He dialed. "Hi! Dar Barish? Yes *sir*. I'm Preston Gerardi and—yeah, Sheriff Dellheim, he did. Thanks. Welcome to San Mateo. Well, the works. Cameras, videos. Everything. We should have, God knows, but no. She wanted to keep the place untainted by the modern era. Built in '07. That's 1907. *Lots*. Gotta fix it. Ok, bring everything you need. Tomorrow. Nine o'clock. Melody. Yes sir, you have my gratitude. See ya in the AM. Bye now."

"Security guy," he said to Cinnah. "Oh, Ok. One more call." He waited. "JoJo! Well, that's sweet, my dear. And Mother would be doing a jig to hear that, right now. Well," he looked around at Cinnah and shrugged in a questioning way, "at this moment, I am on the way to the hospital. Yep, they managed to pull it off. She might be flyin' over your head, my head, right now, throwin' things down at me. Why?

Because I do. The way it is. Ok. Listen, tomorrow, can you feed about—I don't know, maybe a dozen. Working men. Mid-morning. At the house. Yep. She's back. Yep, yep. Yep. Never forget that Trick or Treat party. JoJo, honey, don't cry. Come on, we have to see. Yes, thank you, my darling. Yes, I'll see you in the morning. Right now, we're arriving at the hospital, JoJo. Gotta go. Many thanks, bye. Bye."

He reached for Cinnah's hand. "I hate calling people."

"You love it." She couldn't resist. "Who's Sarah?" He smiled, and removed his hand from hers.

"Sarah," he said, "is the most annoying person on earth. You'll see. Twenty-five years a cop at the *Houston* Police Department and she's still a bubble head." He waited a half-instant, his call to Sarah was going through, and then *sans* charm, without a Texas twang, he merely grumbled to his sister, "Hey. Not yet. Gettin' there. Sarah, I will. I already *have*. Yes, we're all set. I didn't mean that. Now. Stop. Stop, Sarah. Just keep it together. One foot in front of the other. You can always go upstairs. Well, but—sure, you're right. Where are ya? *What?* Do you think that's a good idea? Nobody said you had to do *that*. You could stay—Ok, Ok. You do what you want. You always do. I understand. What? Her laptop. Well, hell fire. Don't worry about it right now. We'll do something. You want to mess with that *today*? Well, tell Fausto. Well, it was. It *is*. Everything is in place. You need to be there at nine. More or less sharp. Ok, Yoli, Magda, and Margaret. Calvert's, Max. Yeah, I got him. We'll get it fixed, or get a new one. Call Max. Tell him what color. Or wood. Whatever style. I don't give a damn. Don't start. Ok, Ok, I'll tell her but you *know* they may not let us see her. Nobody. I mean *me—us—civilians*, visitors, outsiders. Listen. Gotta go. You too. *Im das Morgan.* About nine. Yeah, yeah, bye."

He patted Cinnah's hand on the console. She gave him a small pleasant smile. "It's nice sometimes not to have to talk a lot," she told him.

Preston raised his hands to heaven. "At last, a woman who understands reason." He frowned. Why did he say *woman*? She'll be all over him. Just shut the hell up.

Cinnah had twice missed the exit to the hospital and was inching through quitting time traffic about to go for a third miss. She was feeling the stress. "I hope they give us masks and gloves. So, what else needs to be done?"

Preston was conflicted. Oddly, he was so grateful that she was still talking to him that he almost couldn't speak, although several unseemly comments did creep into his mind. Well, she had missed that turn yet again, was driving in a circle. *Whatever.* Without planning, he said to her, "You ever read that book, about the French Revolution, 'It was the worst of times, it was the best of times'? Yeah? Is that a nod? Well. What is it? *Tale of Two Cities.* Well. Today, Miss Cinnah—right? Your name is C-i-n-n-a-h, true? Cinnah. I got up like any morning. Had no idea on earth it would be possibly the worst day in my life and at the same time possibly the best day of my life. You see. Believe me, Preston Gerardi does not meet someone like you every day, not in a decade, not in a quarter century. Not in a half a—"

Cinnah had pulled to a stop for a young soldier's greeting and they listened to his request for documentation. He stared hard at them over his army-issued mask but went to his guard platform for Mr. Gerardi and his driver's pre-authorized paperwork, and upon giving them masks and gloves and a squirt each of sanitizer, and directions, the soldier saluted and wished them both a bless' day. They were in. Faus Dellheim had done it again, after all. Now they had only to find the appropriate hospital ER entrance, one of three. Preston told Cinnah, "If we keep being patient and long-suffering, we'll be alright. Oprah says, 'Turn your wounds into wisdom.'" He nodded at her. "Oprah," he said, controlling his breathing, his voice, "really."

"Oprah," Cinnah whispered and Preston had to lean in to hear her, "she has a way of turning everything into herself, I'm not judging, but I do judge. Oprah is like that old song, '...lookin' for love in all the wrong places...'"

Preston's mind was firing away and he wanted to follow every flash with a cryptic remark but all he could do was force himself to remain totally silent.

"But you are right about one thing," she was saying when Preston could hear again, "we certainly have a lot of territory to cover. Things to discuss, I mean."

Preston blinked—back in the game, he wiped fake sweat from his forehead and gushed in fake surprise. "Thank goodness, I was afraid you meant property."

Cinnah frowned. "What property? Why would I care anything at all about your property?"

"Exactly," he agreed. "Especially when we're not even married yet, not engaged. Yet."

"Thank heaven!" Cinnah hoped she didn't sound rude.

"Then, can we go steady," he asked. "What do you say?"

"I say, excuse me, you are insane, you need to be locked up, but Ok, since we are locked into this fun house, this snake pit, together, today, only, you may go steady with me—"

"Are you actually saying that you *will* go steady with me," he asked, trying to hide the silly delirium he felt. It was long past him now, his search for her fatal flaw. Whatever it was. Is. Now he clutched the main thing he had left, hope. He committed himself to hope, *hope*.

"Whichever," she said and gave him another face that clearly said, "You are an idiot."

They passed the helicopter pad and parked in a place still reeking of fuel fumes, oddly reminiscent of disaster, past or future. Preston and Cinnah were exhausted from their private ordeal, but their public one was just beginning. Standing, out of the car, she was tall enough to make it possible for them to look at each other almost eye-to-eye. After asking directions from every human they saw, the two of them arrived, by foot, at the correct ER entrance where they were sternly but politely halted. Preston felt certain he could see through the glassed entrance walls into one of several trauma bays where an obviously newly arriving patient, swathed in a white covering, was under the attendance of eight or ten, possibly a dozen, medics, doctors, in hospital pastels. It was his mother. He knew it. Either it was Lynsey Ann, having arrived by helicopter minutes before, or it was one very tall young unfortunate soldier with a full head of curly white-and-grey hair.

A military Chaplain, in camouflage uniform, wearing a mask and gloves, came to speak to them through an opening on the other side of the curtain of glass. He was Army Captain Dung and, after assuring them he would soon return, he brought a nurse, garbed all around in protective attire. They were ready, and together they told Preston and Cinnah the trauma team had received Mrs. Gerardi's medical records. She had been given blood, was on oxygen and was receiving liquids. She had fractured four ribs left side and had deflated her left lung. The plan was to insert a second drain into her chest cavity, possibly three drains, and extract blood and fluids and air, to prevent pneumonia. Her shoulder injury could wait but it was thought it would not require surgery right away. Probably physical therapy. Later, on the other hand, she would shortly undergo surgery to her jaw. That was less strategic but still necessary. All else seemed to be in order. She had various bruises and cuts, areas of broken skin. She had received blunt force trauma to both kidneys, and they were going to be monitoring that; if necessary, she could be put on immediate dialysis. In order to help her body recover, the team has agreed to put Mrs. Gerardi into a state of induced coma, temporarily, 24-hours or a few days.

Preston told Captain Dung and the nurse, "She also recently had her gallbladder removed." The nurse checked her list. "Noted," she said as Preston swayed awkwardly, drunkenly—and to the amazement of all, his six-foot-three, 215 pound body began a slow slide to the sidewalk outside the ER's glass entrance. Nearby soldiers and attendants who had grabbed him, now kindly were attempting to stand him up. Cinnah clutched Preston's arm, and pulled herself close to him, a stanchion for his weakness. The nurse, no rank obvious, but likely a Captain or Major, had not yet finished with her report on Lynsey Gerardi's condition and she chose to ignore Preston. The man had obviously been drinking. She and the Vietnamese-born American Captain with a small golden cross velcroed on his chest simply stood, going over their notes, since they, behind their glass, could not reach for Preston, touch him, or support him. There was nothing they could do. They were across the bridge, beyond the pale, locked into the busy, if not chaotic, other side of the center.

But, since time is fleet, and with Preston at least now on his feet again, though wobbly and not completely attentive, but

67

closer to Cinnah than he ever thought to be, the nurse turned her total attention to the distraught younger blonde wife and said, "We are also very concerned about your mother-in-law because it is believed she may have been exposed to COVID-19. She will be tested, of course, and monitored and for now, we will keep her in absolute isolation in the ICU. When they are ready to move her there. She seems to be strong for her age, and we hope she will recover in time. We will be doing our very best for her, and so because of her condition and because of the threat of COVID-19, you understand, we can't allow her visitors."

"But how could that be? COVID?" Preston roared. "She doesn't go any *anywhere*. She stays at home. She's been self-isolating for weeks, for ten days at least in a row."

The nurse exchanged a few words with the nodding chaplain and assured the Gerardi couple that the team working on COVID connections would be calling and tracking their mother's recent moves. The nurse looked at them suspiciously, it seemed to Preston. And again she expressed her assurances, her hopes for recovery and, excusing herself, walked away.

The chaplain apologized for keeping them standing. He checked to see if Preston's cell number was correct. He told them, "Your mom is in very good hands, the best in the nation. Remember she is in God's hands. Go home and take care of your family. It does you or your family no good for you to try to be here every day. She is being cared for. Go home, take care of each other and take care of your family. Take care of yourselves." Through the port in the glass wall, he passed them his card and said that he would be praying for them and their mom. They were dismissed.

The two of them stumbled along together and plopped down at the nearest empty outdoor bench they found. Cinnah, sitting with one supportive arm around on Preston's back and with her other hand waving in circles to match her speech, was definitely in his space. She was so close to him, they were breathing each other's air, had been while inside her car, and COVID was now something they might share, if they had to. Preston listened, really listened, as she spoke to him the way she would to her eight-year-old son Kevin, reassuring, encouraging, calming him.

It was the Golden Hour, the extended time when, in Lynsey's case, the quality of medical treatment might or might not keep her alive. For Preston and Cinnah, it was 19:45, military time, Daylight Savings, the golden hour, the last sixty minutes *before* the coming of the spring Texas sunset, when the light is warmer, softer and the low angle of the sun offers longer shadows and a more revealing pattern in nature, faces, eyes. On the bench during their gold-splashed hour of the worst day, the best day, Preston was youthful, kind-hearted. Cinnah was enthralling and serene. She felt very positive about the future.

"How far," she asked him, "do you think it is to that hotel you mentioned earlier today?"

Chapter eight ~ the Sheriff's Wife

"I love thee freely, as men strive for right"

How do I love thee? Let me count the ways

-Elizabeth Barrett Browning

The garage, attached to the elegantly aging fifties-style ranch house, rumbled awake, belching out a cacophony of metal straining against metal. Then, silence. One, two, three, and a four, the kitchen door crashed open and a large naked man of uncertain age stormed into the kitchen.

"Faust, damn it to hades," the lady of the house yelled, "you got to *stop* doing that! You scare me to death, how often must I tell you—what if there were people in here, my friends, sheriff or no sheriff. You want people, somebody, to see you like *that?"*

He continued his march, although it was becoming more like a slide, and yelled back at her, "There are no *people*. Nobody's gonna be here. We're in the middle of a fucking pandemic, there are no friends gonna be in this house, no visitors. I just dumped my fucking coronavirus clothes"— he looked down—"except for my socks, sorry. I'm going to take a shower."

"Faust," she screamed.

"*What?*' he yelled.

"Stop saying 'fucking' all the time."

He muttered to himself and she—Shirley Jones Dellheim—laughed. "You know, Faus," she shouted after him, "you remind me of my little sister. When she wanted to be real bad, she'd say, 'Devil, devil, devil.' She was cute. You are not."

Shirl collected clean "unders" for her husband, pajama bottoms, shirt, bright eye-popping socks, each one, each side covered with a dancing hula girl. She lined up slippers and grabbed his comfortable old "Clayton Williams for Governor" windbreaker. After a hot shower, you don't want to catch a chill.

While he dressed, she lay on her side of the bed, totally exhausted. He said, "I guess you heard?"

Shirl clutched the side of the bed and pulled herself half-up. Blinking her eyes against her fading dizziness, she asked, "How is Lynsey doing?"

"We got her on a life-flight to Ft. Sam Houston. Can you believe Preston Gerardi actually wanted me to drive him down there? And, just a little bit ago, a young man showed up with his grandfather. Looking for her, for Lynsey. The fellow called me from her house; they didn't know what was going on, but Alvin Lopez brought them on over to the department. The grandpa, it seemed, went to high school with Lynsey. Go figure, I don't know what's goin' on, but he took it hard. I thought we were going to have to life-flight *him* out of here. He wanted to get on the road to San Antonio right now, but finally he accepted they weren't going to let anybody see her. We offered to put 'em in a hotel, but they said they aw-ready had a room, just be in touch with them. But, you know, Shirl, the thing is, I don't think she'll make it. They really did a number on her, the bastards."

"I heard. But any news since she got there?"

"Preston said he'd call, but not so far. Ended up, he got some reporter to drive him. I might call him."

"In a bit. Did you hear about Gina? Gina Greene. She had her baby today. A little girl. As of this afternoon late. And Fausto, she's going to name the baby *Lynsey*. Lynsey *Ann*." Shirl reached out to her husband and he scooted to her side and they cried, the sheriff cried real tears, and they sat, holding each other until Shirl pushed him away, "Get off of me. Good grief. Let's just go—go, eat your supper. Get it over with. All this has been horrible. So. Don't you start makin' *me* cry. If I start, believe me, I will *never* fucking stop."

~~~

Sheriff Fausto Dellheim plopped into his easy chair, yanked at the lever, and flopped back so he could stretch out. "Good din-din, Shirl. So, what else you got that's going on today in the world of news and horror?"

Shirl occupied the sofa, her territory, "Prince Philip has it, the coronavirus. He's in his nineties." She spun through her cell phone. "I guess it's everywhere now. Poor old thing. Those royals have no life."

Faus grunted, smiling. Shirl was a living doll.

"World Health Organization—that's the WHO, nobody likes them. WHO says the United States has the potential to become 'the global epicenter of the pandemic.' Whatever. No wonder nobody likes 'em."

'We're all gonna die, all gonna kick the bucket."

"No, Faus, wait now, they say New York City is the *epicenter*, *the epicenter* of the global epicenter of the pandemic. New York City has more than 25,000 cases and that's doubling every three days. Everybody wants more testing, tests, tests, tests. Let's see, some idiots in Kentucky had a party to welcome in the coronavirus, now they've all got it. Oh, big whoop, the 2020 Olympics are finally canceled. Fashion industry *blah blah*. Tom Hanks and his wife are having a voter registration party."

Shirl put her cell aside. "Who do they think they are? What I want to know is—they were over in Australia, right? When they got it, COVID. Were they over there working with the poor, setting people up with jobs? Were they there helping with sick kids in the hospital? Were they developing meds for sick people? No. They were making some trashy movie. Why? Because they don't *know* anything, can't do anything, haven't discovered anything. Now they recovered from Coronavirus, but tell me—how did they get a flight back to the US? I thought the airlines were down, no? Am I wrong? Well, must have opened up so freaking Tom Hanks and his wife could get back to Hollywood, the intellectual capital of the world, so they could tell us what to do."

"You're a bitter woman, Shirl Dellheim."

Shirl went back to her phone. "Says here DJ-Nice held a party on Instagram for 100,000 people—one of them was Michelle Obama. Now how can they tell? A hundred thousand people, my—"

"Now you're gettin' obnoxious," Faus quipped.

"Some people are so tired of staying at home, they are dressing up in evening clothes to take the trash out."

"Now why is that?"

'Bored. Crazy. You know, Faus, I feel kind of ashamed."

"Yeah, Shirl? Why is that?"

"Ok, like back during Viet Nam, people were nasty, ugly, protesting, maybe for a reason. Maybe not. Then Desert Storm, again not everybody was involved but most people pulled together. Then 9-11, everybody was hurt, shocked, but we had this togetherness."

"Shirl, for about ten minutes, right after 9-11, next day just about, they had lawyers fightin' over who's gonna get a lifetime of money, the bigger house, free college. Forget the soldiers killed right after that in Iraq and Afghanistan, their families, what do they get if their sponsor gets killed? What, maybe ten thousand? Now what you are about to say is that people, the American people, are acting like jerks over this virus, but the truth is, my dear, they—we—have always acted like jerks."

"Today is worse. Saying they are losing their freedoms because they have been asked to stay at home *during a virus.* Lucky they have homes, lucky they aren't in London during the war and are asked to go to the bomb shelter—to save their lives."

"I don't know, but I get it, and I'm fed up." Faust slammed his copy of the *San Mateo Argus* on his chair arm. "I'm fed up. Damn stupid *Argus.* Damn party line."

"You are? You're fed up, Mister Sunlight and Handshakes, Mister Goodwill? *Why*, all of a sudden?"

"I see it, been seeing it for a while. People are just, I don't know. Talk to some of the teachers. These kids are different. Look at them on Spring Break! Bunch of drunk brats. The ones before these kids were no different. Wimpy, selfish. Sorry, Shirl. We idiot Americans have raised two generations of arrogant SOBs, but you can't *say* that. You know why, Shirl? Because our generation raised 'em. We know a lot of people who do not want to hear it. Because they raised these jerks." He yanked the handle on the side of his chair and flopped upright.

"When I was in Viet Nam—and I didn't want to be there, I was 19. I wanted to be playing football for Wake Forest, or A&M, or at the university up the road. I didn't want to go die in 'Nam, but you know what happened that season, in the fall of the year 1970, when I was in Nam, we were in Cambodia, actually—there were *two* airplane crashes in the states that year, one crash killed 20-30 people on board a flight from Wichita State, maybe a dozen were players. About a month later, Shirl, another *different* crash wiped out 75 people from Marshall University in West Virginia. Listen to this: Just about maybe fifty young football players from two different football teams, and others, coaches and all, *killed.* No Viet Cong, no Charlie, just guys my age. Killed. Guys. Who, like me, just wanted to play football."

"Oh, I'm sorry, Faus," Shirl said. "I am just so sad to hear that. Very sad. Wasn't there a movie about Marshall?"

"Yeah," Faust said, "I heard that. Say. We got any chocolate ice cream left? You want some? No. No, no. You stay. I'll get it. You're not saying anything? Yeah, we're in quarantine of sorts. But we can have ice cream. We're part of the me generation, right? Me want, me have."

"Me too, bring me some."

~~~

Shirl sat up. "Ice cream hits the spot. I'd like some more, but I'll skip it. You too. But you know what, Faus," she said, "when you come slidin' in here, naked as a jaybird, reminds me of that guy, what's his name? In the movie? Comes sliding in on socks and then begins dancing around. Not Tom Hanks, thank goodness. *Ted Cruz.*"

Faus chuckled, "No, darlin' girl, Ted Cruz is our senator, has a little 'salt and peppa' beard right now. You're thinking of Tom Cruise in 'Risky Business.'"

"You know, Faus, for some reason, I can't remember 1970. Where was I? You were in Viet Nam, and I must have been in 9th grade. Junior High, back *then*, but that year, the next, I remember TV would show the actual battles. At suppertime. People did not like that. People have always been selfish. And the TV people *loved* to interview angry soldiers, soldiers smoking marijuana, everything in disarray. A bit of mutiny for the folks back home. I was young, what did I know? Listen, Faus, I hope talking, remembering all that, doesn't upset you."

"I know towards the end of the war what went on. Some people were saying 'ten more years.' It's a wonder the troops didn't go into a real frenzy. Talk about *mutiny.*"

76

Shirl was getting worked up again. "We used to believe what was on the news really happened. Now it seems like they put things on TV, online, that they *want* to make happen. I remember when the news said San Mateo had just had its *first* carjacking, like, oh sure, more carjackings are comin' up. And they were."

Faus said, "Damn media. Back when we were in 'Nam—we were on our own, separate from people back in the states— but you could just take it for granted that your buddies were there for you, and you for them. It was understood. There was a loyalty, Shirl. You know, one time I remember we had this kid who was lost. We were actually in Bu Dop Province, edge of Cambodia. We were searching for weapon caches, papers, maps, whatever, and the fuckers popped up and fired on us. We had three killed, two wounded, and our one guy missing, unaccounted for. Well, see, the Cav—you know, the 1st Cavalry—had discovered this giant PAVN supply cache, the *People's* Army, *North* Viet Nam, damn Commies, had tons of stuff stocked, ammunition, rockets, equipment, all kinds. Shirl, listen to me: I saw this with my own eyes. PAVN, the Commies, had *General Motors vehicles, brand new ones,* now how do you account for that, I wonder. Tell me how American damn trucks came to be in the hands of the North Vietnamese army, the Socialist Republic of Vietnam, the Commies, Ho Chi Minh's forces, the SOBs we were fighting. Some day, the truth is going to come out, Shirl, *some* day. There were dirty rich families gettin' richer, working both sides, on our blood, our boys' lives. And some of those families, I'll say, were *presidential*. May God grant us proof, Shirl. *The truth has to come out.* I can't even stand to see their pictures. And now they're dyin' off, oh, what accolades, and now we have new filth, new rich, with political power, so fucking evil, Shirl." Faus struggled to his feet, breathing hard.

"Anyhow, *this* is why guys get PTSD, or call it what it is, outrage. Intellectual and moral outrage, just pure rage, and you can't carry that or you'll get carted away to the loony bin and throw a massive coronary or make the famous headlines the news loves the next day. No, Shril, I tell you PTSD is about finding the dirt, the lies. It's not just explosions, not just gettin' shot at or steppin' on—"

"*Fausto,*" Shirley screamed. "*Stop.* Don't go there. Don't. We are having Coronavirus. Some other day, I'll help you. We'll go around to libraries, visit people. We can investigate, but not *now*. Please, be calm. We have to be ready to help the Gerardi family, the city. You need to call the media in tomorrow. Bring healing. Give a talk. Think about that. Not Viet Nam. I'll help you. I will, I will. With Viet Nam, when the time is right, we'll investigate, I promise, we'll do it, I'll even drive the get-away car."

Faus smiled. He sat on the edge of a straight back chair. "Yep, *Miss Jonesy,* as we used to call you back in the day—when you were in the office—you're right. All that is for another day. I'm Ok. Living with me must be hell. I just wanted to tell you, one good thing. Back in Cambodia. Back when we had that lost soldier, Ok? We had been looking for documents, lists, maps, all that, just before they fired on us, and then *immediately*, they skedaddled. The word came to withdraw. Now this kid, he was just one of us, wasn't nobody. Wasn't a damn Kennedy or some Hollywood brat. I guess it was mutiny. We said no, we're not leaving him. He's one of us. We were not gonna leave him."

"What happened? I'm almost afraid to ask."

"Well. That place, I tell you, Shirl, was all rubber trees, really thick undergrowth, vines, bamboo. You couldn't find the

Taj Mahal, but we were crawling and digging through that mess looking for that kid."

"So, what happened? Did y'all find him?"

"We did! We found him. He'd been on the run, moving, running, when he tripped on some vines. Hit his head on a mango tree or something, He was Ok. We found him."

"Well, what happened to him?" she asked and Fausto muttered, "Same as anybody else."

Shirl frowned. "Your stories always stop where they should start. What's the point?"

Faus hooted. "Ha. I thought we were relaxing after a day from hell, talking about the war. And Covid. Does everything have to have a point?"

"Well, I would think so, yes. What became of this fellow?"

"Shirley, let it go." And Shirl made to zip her lips and toss away the key.

Later, after the sheriff crawled into bed next to his wife, he kissed her shoulder and said, "Hey, don't go away mad."

Shirley smiled. "Just go away." She pushed his chest with her fingertips. "You better not be naked again. Move over. Six foot rule."

"I am not *neked*. I've been thinking. This is a pretty tough deal for you. Being quarantined, mostly. We have groceries delivered, so you don't go shopping. You don't have the things you usually do. Or go to."

"The cleaning lady doesn't come anymore," Shirl began in a sing-song. "The milkman doesn't come anymore. The ice man doesn't come anymore."

"Yardman *still* comes. Mailman. But listen, anybody, but anybody, comes to this house, you don't answer or if you know them, make 'em wear masks, and gloves. There's boxes in the chair on the porch. I'm gonna have to see about getting you a box of booties. Slip over their shoes. And then, I am always gone or too tired to poop. It's a big house; you don't have any fun. All you do is work."

"*No booties.* And, I'd like to think my life is a little more fruitful than the way you describe. This is my *choice.* I have agreed to stay home because I have a so-called underlying condition. So, doesn't everyone have an underlying so-called condition? I stay home because I choose to live, most days. No, I like our old house on Limestone Drive. It's not like Gerardi's house, but I like it. And I am not going to the doctor's or hospital, or the the nail salon, but it's Ok. Now, is Lynsey going to be Ok? While ago, you said she's done for, but why? Oh! I forgot to remind you to call Preston. Too late?"

"Eleven o'clock. Yeah. That miserable old bastard. He would have called if she got worse. And now, sister Sarah Gerardi from Houston has pranced onto the scene. You know she almost literally broke my back trying to get a ride on that chopper—that I had to fight like cats and dogs to get for poor old Lyns."

"Very proud that you did, good job. High *five.*" Faus gave his wife a very high, almost unreachable, high five.

"*Stinker.*"

Faus continued. "You know, during my time, I have responded to many a home break-in. Most times houses are empty when it happens." Shirley sighed tragically. "We in law enforcement do everything in our power to console the victims that, whatever it takes, we'll apprehend whoever's responsible. Sometimes that means staying there through your shift just to give them a sense of security. We get the fire department guys to board up whatever the entry point is to be sure the place feels safe again. Sometimes when you're in the house you can feel how violated the victims feel. Imagine seeing your underwear and intimate belongings strewn around on the floor and bodily excrement on your bed."

Shirl hissed, "Can you be any more explicit?"

"Well, it's just stuff, sure, but the stolen goods might include jewelry from family members long gone, irreplaceable items. But today inside Lynsey's old house—it nearly killed me. I knelt by the side of her, she was crumpled and bleeding and, Shirl, my heart broke. It did. Let me get a drink of water." He gulped from a water bottle, offered it to Shirl who declined.

"You know, Lynsey and I have a history. I was new to the department, not long back from 'Nam. I was the idiot they called on to go to that house and tell that woman her son, a beautiful smart kid, on his way in a car to Notre Dame, that her boy had been killed in Indiana. She nearly died.that day. A Sunday. All the other kids. It was a very bad time and then almost exactly one year later, like it was planned, Shirl, her second son, a really special boy, nice—I always suspected he'd go be a priest, but he had a girlfriend, the grandmother of Gina. Sounds like Peyton Place. It was horrendous. Once again I was eye-to-eye with a mother, that same mother, telling her that her second boy was dead."

"So tragic, Faus."

"And today, I had to tell her *third* son, old Preston, that his mother might not make it, but at least we got her to the trauma center. All we can do is hope and wait."

Shirl asked, "This Cesar guy, that died? That Cora shot? Did you know him?"

"No, just that he was a druggie, mostly buying, not selling. But, my girl, guess what? I forgot to tell you."

"What? Tell me. I could use some good news."

"The other guy," Faus says, "named Noe Alejandro—" and Shirl breaks in, "Alejandro with a 'j'? Not Ann Alejandro's son! Don't tell me. He was one of them? The family must feel so ashamed. She's an ER nurse, Faus. She used to work for Lynsey."

"Yeah, that's right. He's gone, bled out on them in the operating room. Or after. Now both bastards are dead."

"I feel sick," Shirl said, reaching for her suede-covered bible. "I'm going to read a little 'Isaiah.' I have been reading Isaiah since when, 1996, still can't make heads-or-tails out of it, but it puts me to sleep."

"Sorry, Shirley, I was talking too much. You go ahead and read. Try to relax. I'm just going to lie here. Most people would say 'lay,' 'I'm going to lay here,' but if you say lay, you have to *lay* something or someone down, someone like Shirley," and he grabbed her.

She screamed. "Stop, seriously. Faus, I think, I am nauseated as hell. The room is spinning. Why don't you just talk to me.

My face feels all stiff—I *am* going to be sick, Faus. Can you get me a wet washcloth? A bucket? I'll wait here. You know I love you, don't you? Faus?"

With no answer from her husband and not enough time had passed for him to have fallen into death by heart attack, Shirley called out, "Faus? I love you. Don't forget the bucket, Ok? Sweetie?"

~~

'Hope you're better," Faus said, "and I meant to tell you, my clothes out in the garage? Don't touch 'em. Don't touch any of my dirty clothes. I'll put them in a plastic bag, take 'em to an industrial cleaner, somewhere. I was everywhere today nobody would want to be."

"Ok, thanks, Faus. And you're wearin' gloves all day, changing them ever so often?"

"Yep, and we're all wearing masks, most of the time."

"I have a girlfriend who posted she went to some office, or nail salon, wearin' her mask—no, not a nail salon, somewhere—and the receptionist was not. Wearing a mask. So my friend asks her if the company didn't direct them to wear masks, and the girl says, 'Oh, yes ma'am, we have 'em. We can wear them if we need to.'"

"My God, will this craziness ever end? I've got Lynsey's laptop in the car."

"What? How come?"

"I have no idea. Crazy thing. I saw that laptop earlier, when we were at the house. Sittin' on the dining room table. Wonder why the bastards didn't steal it. No. Think somebody else took it, today, right under our nose, then maybe they felt bad and dumped it off at the hospital and, fortunately, it had her name on it, so somebody called us. I'll give it to Preston in the morning."

"I wouldn't want to be Preston, or Sarah, trying to sleep in that house tonight," Shirl said.

'You know what I was telling you while ago about Viet Nam, when we went into Cambodia? Well, now I remember that kid's name. He was Ronald Smoot. I couldn't remember Smoot or Small," Faus lied. "He went back to Oklahoma City and worked in a barber shop. Heard now he owns a string of them all over Oklahoma."

"Good for him, around Oklahoma City?"

"What? Oh, yeah, Oklahoma City, all over. No, but the point of *that* story was us hanging together to find his ass. What I meant is, I never had that feeling of solidarity again. Things, people, changed. Back when I joined the department 100 years ago—actually, Shirl, it's been 48 fucking years, sorry—but we still had an old fashioned way of doing things. We took the drunks home. We only ticketed out-of-towners, and we never hurt a fellow deputy. Over the years, the philosophy changed. Everything has to be by-the-book. You have to document every damn thing you do, or say, or what's said to you. Guys lost the ability to commiserate with the public.

"And the public, maybe they lost respect. Used to, you'd arrive at a fight or argument between a couple of belligerents and whatever bullshit you used would calm things down, but *then*, now, by-the-book, the minute you start questioning, taking names and phone numbers, whatever goodwill there might have been going on with a couple of nothing nitwits, it all evaporates."

He said, "I 'pologize, I'm really on a talking jag. But you get fed up. You expect the lawyers and 'the officers of the court' to hate you, but it got where your 'brother officers,' your own people, would stab you in the back, report you, to promote themselves or step over you.

"I don't know. I can't tell you how hardened you get to life and people, most of them, just trying to hang on. Somebody's always trying to bring you down.

"You know, Shirl, I am almost thrilled when a call comes in that some jerks set fire to a bunch of toilet paper in the boys' restroom. Of course, you're always thinking disaster—one pissant fire, the whole dang school blows up. But jerk wad kids, no, that's almost a pleasure."

Shirl took his hand. "Yes, I know. Honey. I see you suffer." She tugged on his hand and placed it over her hip bone and asked him, "What do you feel?"

"Something nice."

"Fausto, I'm trying to tell you. Look at me, really look."

Faus lifted his head, squinted at her. "Are you crying, honey?" And he pulled her into a hug.

Shirley said, "It's like I am complaining and I'm not, not to you, never to you, but Lynsey Gerardi is not the only one who lost two sons. *We did. I did.*"

And now it was Faus' turn. He was crying. Their boys, twins, had lived less than a day.

Shirl whispered fiercely into his ear, "If they had lived, they would have gone to Spring Break. They would be out there, dancing and fishing and throwing ropes around COVID, and bringing it home, and I wouldn't even care."

Faus remembered the hospital bed, Shirley smiling, holding both babies, wrapped tight in blue striped blankets, little faces peeking out. She was so thrilled, sweet-talkin' them, not even aware the smaller one, the one Shirl called Marc, was already dead. Their bigger, first born son, Rhydian, lived only an hour more. Those babies, with their mother's Welsh nonconformist names, were a wonder, gone so soon.

Faus said, "If our boys were still alive today, they would be 42 years old, the prime of life. I wish they were. They could do everything. I would forgive anything."

She asked, "Would they have been in law enforcement?"

"Maybe builders, in business together."

"Yeah, I'd like it if they worked together. Maybe they'd have a dental practice. A law firm. By now, their kids would be wanting to go to spring break."

"Nope," he said. "Too young. Having a sheriff granddad, they're too young for that nonsense."

"I like talking about them," Shirl said, "but give me your hand. Here, on my hip. No silliness, Faus. Can you tell? I'm wasting away, I have lost more than 30 pounds since Christmas. It's March 25th. In three months. I almost weigh what I did when we got married. But no, I don't expect you to fix the world for me. Being married to you, I've always felt like a little girl." She laughed lightly, "'Thou art strong,' and I am forever the weak one. I want that to change, except now, I really am the weak one, getting weaker, fading away, and now I think I need you to, not *do* things for me. But do them *with* me, can you understand? Tell me you understand. Help me."

Faus said, "I am capable of it. But here's what I want to tell you"—Shirley moaned faintly—"I am 70 years old—Marc and Rhydian would be 42 years and three months of age—I have been with the department 47 years, no, 49 years. I can stay until I'm 75, and this year, as you may dreadfully recall, is election year. Time to roll out the signs and placards, empty out the old storage shed.

"Now, now, listen," he said, "not much has been said about the campaign since mid-January because of COVID, and I don't know what the hell the governor will do, but I was thinking, if you agree—I don't have an opponent, but I'm pretty sure I could easily find a replacement on the ticket."

Shirl let out a little scream.

Faus continued, giving one of the most important speeches of his life. "I have someone in mind. And come November, well, January, we're free of Sheriff Dellheim."

"What are you saying? Really?" Shirl really felt like a small silly child. Was Santa Claus real? The Easter bunny left her something? What? She bloomed, then shrank back. "Have you thought about it? You can do this? Walk away all during COVID?"

"Honey, who knows? We can't plan for what might happen. Out there. We have to plan for ourselves. And if we have to suffer from the virus, then I will do the suffering right here, quarantined, with you. Plant a garden, have our own watermelons. But maybe we can travel too, city to city, if we plan it. Visit around."

Faus couldn't stop talking. "We can do some research. Like you were saying. Visit some old boys. And try that Ancestry-dot-nutcakes thing. Find our Roots. Go two-steppin' and do a little *Do Si Do, Allemande Left.* What do you say? There are other people who can do this job. There's only one of you and one of me. Whatever it is we do, come November, we do it together."

"Thank you, Fausto. It's one-thirty in the morning. Nobody would believe we stayed up this late talking. I know how hard it is for you to give up the next five years, and I look forward to the days—the *days,* Fausto—the trips that we might take, things we will do together. Thank you, my love. Thank you, for this time."

She gave him a long goodnight kiss, and had him join her in saying the Our Father. Then they slept. Shirl did.

Faust stayed awake, trying not to face his worries. Damn shitstorm coming, with Lynsey and Cora. Somebody's gonna sue. Watch for it. Stupid COVID. Got to pull it together. Something's very wrong. Gotta talk to Shirl about the boys more. Can't settle anything, we need answers, but something's wrong, something crooked has been going on all this time, since fifty years ago in Viet Nam.

"And I am going to find out what, and expose it," he said to himself, "or I will die tryin' to."

Chapter nine ~ the Cleansing

"...the world's more full of weeping..."

The Stolen Child

W.B. Yeats

Thursday, the day after the attack on Lynsey, Sarah Gerardi, awake at seven AM, late for her, looked around herself at the covers on her borrowed bed and shook her head and groaned, "No, can't be." Nauseated yet oddly gratified, she knew she had to resolve this dilemma of her own making. And quickly. Those years in Houston, she had lived in the eye of other people's frequent and on-going storms, but now, this was her own doing, mostly her own doing, like 95 percent. A disaster, still. At a time when Mother needed her full attention. She thought of Preston, stupid jerk. She reached for her cell to call him. He likely had stayed over in San Antonio. Crazy idiot. Did he think the hospital might call him to come immediately? Well, maybe.

Answer, answer. Preston, answer the damn phone. He was scaring her to death. She checked her text messages. Found one, sent last night. Ok, Ok. Says Mother is in trauma ICU. Holding on. Will be tested—*what?* For COVID. "Dear Father God," Sarah said aloud. She had already agreed to meet Preston at the house this morning—he had arranged for a cleaning team and repairmen, and so on. The front door was, well, carpentered shut. *Carpentered?* Is there such a word? Who knows? It was seven AM. She had two hours before meeting her mother's cleaning ladies—Yoli, and Yoli's niece, little chippy from Mexico, and one other, but what the heck is her name? Her identity was obscured, but not her face, or her manner, her way of being. *Ha.* Sarah snuffed a smile. And her name was? Inside an empty box in Sarah's mind. This had been happening more and more lately. Words, *right there,* and she couldn't speak them. And names? Gone with the breeze. Wind. Frustrating. But after cancer or a major crisis, it was normal. The after-effects of cancer, she had found, made you lose self-esteem. Sometimes she worried, for a few minutes, not for long, that her chief, ancient old Jed James, at the Houston PD, actually at the science center, had noticed a crack in her confidence, and it wasn't her health and COVID that concerned him. He would have told her. He would have, wouldn't he? He would have told her. Not just decided.

So, Mother's favorite cleaning team, the third member of Squad Two, being still a mystery—her mother and Preston "managed" *a dozen* or more cleaning squads. Groups of two or three workers that Mother called *Squads.* Good grief. But Squad Two and some fellows, carpenters always aware of the next thing needing to be repaired around the old place, would be at the house this morning. Cleaning and repairs. Preston had assured her a security system guy would be there to install home indoor-outdoor security cameras. Sarah spoke, as if someone could hear her, or answer back, "I want cameras in the back of the house, over the tennis court, around the garage and one, at least, facing the gate to the cemetery." Since we basically all live there. Might as well see who's coming and going, messing around. Our dad, Yuri, and Hollis. My turn, she thought morosely. Whatever.

Or, Mother's. Bury us together. Or not, since COVID. Remember? Do you?

Today she'd tell the security fellow, at the house, "I want more cameras than Hollywood." I feel rotten, so I'll be a smart aleck. Preston said he had set it up with Calvert's Locksmiths—and Sarah's mind wandered away, on its own feet, to Stevie Calvert, long ago, and a September dance one night on the basketball court. The sudden rain storm, silly, crazy kids, soaking wet at the stupid but thrilling (at the time) Back-to-School dance, supposed to be the source of non-date dates, relationships, secret moments of hand-holding, for the entire year, both semesters.

Sarah and her older sister Jewel had attended St. Pius X High School for girls. It was, back then, a fairly new school and Sarah's class was the school's celebratory 10th year class, "celebratory," perhaps to prove St. P's was still in business as (at that time) many Catholic schools, new ones, old ones, had closed. Were closing. Each year, as her class inched closer to graduation time, the bigger the deal they became. Catholics love to celebrate, jubilees, anniversaries, festivals, feast days and still might do so in some of Houston's "satellite cities," Columbus, La Marque, Rosenberg, El Campo, *Flatonia*. Yep, Houston was still Sarah's area of concern. Twenty-five years is a long time. It was her city.

The morning after her mother's attack, Sarah turned her mind to bitter memories and smiled at herself, looking back, like some old granny. She remembered how Catholic schools in the big city—in Houston, that is—had begun closing, decade after decade, most recently bowing to state-funded Charter Schools. Why not? Catholicism itself was still running strong as a "claimed religion," but there is a difference between claimed and practiced, and so perhaps some dried-up Papist will arise out the archival ruble and slowly, painfully, open a Roman Catholic museum, hold tours, with fresh-faced docents explaining the mysteries of feasts days, CYA, youth sports, Holy Communion, the Eucharist. Confession. And the quaint concept of purgatory, once considered a great topic for unfettered discussions.

Sarah was one of the disheartened but unnumbered "young" yet still active Catholics in the US, but she—like mother, so like daughter—held to tender memories of what she liked to think of as early days in the church, Catholic schools in the late 1970s, when long-legged girls secretly shortened their uniform skirts every month or so. They might have gotten away with it if short girls hadn't tried the same trick, and they didn't have the legs to spare, you understand. Add *that* to your Papist museum tours. The shrinking Catholic girl uniform skirt. And school dances with nuns in attendance.

The year of Sarah's back-to-school dance when a rainstorm drenched the dancers as well as the sitters on the wall, the nuns were no doubt first to jump ship. That year, she had been a sophomore. Sarah shuttered.

How did Mother allow a 14-year-old—*not even close to 15*— to go to a dance, with boys? She even drove us. Forced us to go. And that night, sophomore year, once they were soaking wet, they got into a boy's car and went to his cousin's house where some girl, a college student still at home, gave three sophomores from St Pius each a dry outfit. Did we keep our underwear on? We were giggling like mad. I remember my bra was soaking wet. No cell phones. We made the decision to go to a strange house and take our wet clothes off, dear God—it could have been a set-up and we would be half-way to Michigan or Mexico before Mother stopped watching "Dynasty" long enough to figure out we were missing. Much less that the highways were flooded.

How weird that someone in authority thought it essential that 14-year-olds find a match. We'd barely had our books issued, purchased. Here's your stack of books, and here's your match—he's only 12 and would rather be at home watching Dynasty with his mom. And then, after the back-to-school mingle, there followed the teenage heartbreaks, the fights. Everybody taking sides. For some, there was new life, the sudden discovery of someone new, someone perhaps from the public school who, like a four-leafed clover, you'd overlooked before. And then, just in time to exchange Christmas presents and find something to wear to the holiday formal, at 15, *he'd break up with you.* Ah, high school. And these kids were such *babies.* But it was fun, it was glorious. Rather glorious.

Wait. Did she *know*? Is that why she sent us? We had been so sad, so droopy. Preston was at home sulking. Immobile. Jewel would be at home crying. And I would have been sitting in front of a mirror somewhere being crabby and as mean as I could be. I was a mean, mean lazy kid. Rude to Mother. I wonder. She almost *forced* us to go to dances, parties, dumped us off at games,

Canteen Teen meetings at church. She even joined the country club *for us* for a while. We had a pool and a tennis court, who needed a snooty country club? I see, I see, said the blind man. She signed us up for every kind of class, bought us *dresses* we made fun of. Why'd she do all that? Because she wanted us to have things, to have—fun? Because—because, she loved us. She loved us. *Far out. Awesome, mamacita.*

Sarah wondered, Stevie Calvert. Would he be at the house, himself? Or would he send an underling? Thinking about the house, Sarah remembered she had a key to the kitchen door. Somewhere.

She wanted to surrender, to beg God. "Only for *her*." God was at times, most times, amazingly good and kind. Other times, he seemed to step aside, as if to say, "This one is on you, kid." Fake news, fake god. The true God, always and ever, was loving. If not, he, she—it, the thing you are talking about—is *not* God. The nature of God is to be loving. An angry outraged God is impossible, although—shocking to some—God is just, and justice can hurt like poison. Tough. He won't bend the river, break the law of nature or logic, not even for you. God won't change other men's will or bring the dead back to life. But he will walk the road with you.

Alone, single, Catholic, and a cop—Sarah accepted the word *cop*—she volunteered each month discussing her faith, and life, with at-risk juvies. It was all so wrong; those kids had been brought up like chickens. Scratch around, don't let *no one* take your chick-chick feed. Damn. She could have worked another ten years easily, maybe fifteen. Now, less than a week back home in San Mateo—this, with Mother. No cases, no work to get absorbed in; Mother comes first. So, Sarah asked God *only* for her mother to be spared the deep pain that victims, especially at age 87—some of them—simply can not endure. Will not survive. In life, we're top of the dog pile, and then, *pow,* that one thing happens. Cancer. Somebody comes with a murderous rusty wrench. And the thing *then* that eats a victim's soul, it's a weak-sick conviction that just shows up and denies all that you are and have been. You know you're a loser, so give up. God, spare Mother that sense of desolation. The shock, the confusion and outrage. Give it to *me*. I will carry the load for both of us. Let her be free of fear. She has withstood and withstood. She's like that stupid house. Grand, but with so many cracks and crevices and with such a fragile foundation. For now, please, just let her stand again, stand tall again.

Two hours, most of the first hour already passing: But now, what was she, the idiotic prodigal daughter, going to do about Marty? Yesterday, in the car. Bad choices.

Later, coming here to his condo. "I did it," she said. "Eyes open. But why, why would I involve him in my life—or did I? And what now?" She reflected on a few major bumps in her no-plan lifeplan, but she was at-one with the assumed psychological status of most men which we may assume is: *Ask me no questions, I will tell you no lies.* Of course. Martin, wherever he is at this hour, is not wading in angst, madly asking himself, what now? What's next? Oh, woe is me, why didn't that work out, or did it? He is not staring into a coffee cup asking himself, oh heavens, oh gosh, oh golly, what is the *meaning* of this? Sarah almost laughed.

Blow-it-off. Martin is the bystander at the scene of an accident. Nose to the window, a nosey witness, never a participant. We'll be friends. I go my way. Free again.

Sarah saw herself from a far distance. Crisply, she told herself: I have a dying mother, a wrecked house, a boring business or four or five to help run, my own health, and soul, to take care of. I don't need a man. Certainly not him.

First to arrive at the house, but unable to produce her key to the back door, the kitchen door, Sarah sat waiting in the Mercedes. She needed to see Sheriff Dellheim about the stolen—or missing—laptop, stupid business. Stolen from her car. Next, second to arrive after Sarah, here came the carpenters, men who could open up the front door—and the guys from, what was it called? Barish's Security Systems. Both the carpenters—sturdy old Max Crawford and how many helpers? Two. And the security business, Barish (two guys) showing up almost at the same moment. *Fishy.* And so, as she waited in her car, it seemed the old place was, in fact, beginning to hum. The carpenters, like busy bees hard at work, pulled at removing the plywood nailed over the entrance. Would the house need a new door? How could it not? Who would choose? Let Preston. Or Mr. Crawford. And the Barish dudes dragging in like bales of wire? Where was Preston when you needed him? We never should have had a door with so much glass in it. You were forced to peek out between the lace like a complete idiot. Or, you were a sitting duck. Too late. You were the victim.

Sarah stepped out of her car, her protection. At the entrance, not looking at what she had seen yesterday, except the trashed door—was it yesterday?—she noticed the men, the workers, had decked themselves out in gloves, masks, booties and various attempts at protective gear. Sarah had a mask, black, and a couple of pairs of gloves in her bag. She dare not mention coronavirus. The whole thing, like Chicken Little's falling sky, like a poison, hung just over her head. COVID. Was it a nightmare? A hoax—end of March and some people were still claiming the virus was a hoax, intended to hurt the President, intended to help the President. Such idiots. This virus—if not a hoax—was already bringing out the eccentrics, the crazed crackpots, preaching that COVID was the end of society on earth. Was it the end? Even if it is, she would like a red door, or bright blue, dark green. Was COVID really the cause of her end to a lifetime in law enforcement? My enemy, damn you, COVID! Leave Mother alone! Leave me, us all, alone.

The cleaning ladies, waving at Sarah, standing at the dining table, had entered the house through the kitchen door. Sarah was bowled over. These women *had a key*. She herself crawled in through a hole in the entrance. How many people in Roeller County held keys to Mother's doors? She made a mental note to talk with the locksmith. Would it be Stevie passing out keys? *This* has to stop. Why not just send out invitations: Come for a Break-in, and a Beating, All Welcome. Open 24-SEVEN. She wondered how many private tours had wandered through in the black of the night? Watching us sleep? Even sleeping here themselves. There was a case she heard about in Houston where a teacher had lived almost the whole school year within the walls of the classroom, the nurse's room, and the janitor's closet.

Sarah was angry. She pulled her face mask down and went out onto the back veranda to brood, for this was a nightmare. She looked down. Her hands were shaking.

The three cleaning ladies from Squad Two crept silently, carrying their supplies to and from the storage room, their heads swiveling side-to-side as if thieves and invaders might still be hiding deeper within the house. Yoli, whose last name is Guzman, was quick to make clear she is *not* from *El Chapo's* drug cartel family in Mexico. As if anybody gave a hoot. But no, she is the leader of Squad Two. She has been cleaning and beautifying Mid-Texas homes for twenty-five years.

"Me too," Sarah thought. "I have been cleaning up for twenty-five years." For Sarah, it was a duty.

For Yoli, it was an escape into a richer, fuller world, where she could make things sparkle and gleam even more, look perfect, where she would prepare a (warm and nice) place where people, the family, could be happy. What could be better? She had a knack—that homeowners were quick to brag about—a pleasing knack for arranging ordinary items into displays of charm. But Yoli, Yolanda, that is, never coveted the things in others' homes. Such things always belonged to the owners.

When work was over, after cleaning three, sometimes four houses in one day, Yoli, happily tired, was satisfied, knowing she'd soon be home where everything also sparkles, and belongs to her alone. Except for her husband Sergio, and Magdalena, her niece, age 20. And the kids, but they were neatniks. Even Magda's little boy was not messy. During the workday, Magda is Yoli's assistant. Today, or most days, they clean and shine in pleasing harmony.

Magda, who grew up in Mexico, seems shy and some might take her as unfocused, but what she lacks in personal drive, she makes up for in pure endurance on the job—Monday through Friday—and on the dance floor late weekend nights at clubs such the Midnite Owl, or Nando's International Club. Magda, the dancer, wears comfy old shoes glued with glitter, and skimpy dresses, for those dance places get hot, hot, *hot*, as do the salsa dance queens of Roeller County.

Magda, no loafer at work Monday through Friday, likes calmly finishing, polishing one area at a time, top to bottom, dusting every square inch, wiping away any sign of occupancy, washing away spills, greasy finger marks, stubborn corner dust, and vacuuming furniture, drapes, and carpets until the deep deep grooves left behind look like tank trails, not vacuum cleaner lines. Magda, a physical person, moving slowly, is always moving. She has one little boy, now in pre-kinder. If anyone asks, she clicks to his pictures on her Apple Watch. Early in her pregnancy, she came to Texas and her son, an American citizen, has an American name, Aiden Elijah Guzman.

Margaret Conant, odd man out on Squad Two, prefers silence, and order. No chit-chat. A bit of a know-it-all, she squints like Peter Falk in *Columbo* and speaks in a faint mutter out of one side of her mouth, like James Dean in *Rebel without a Cause*. She wears her thin brown hair in a ponytail, pops the collars of her work shirts up and, if she happens to like you, will invite you to call her Garet. The thing about Margaret that makes her almost famous in house cleaning circles, is that she is fast and there is no job beneath her. She could do Lynsey's entire downstairs, by herself, in the time it takes the other two to finish two bathrooms and a large kitchen. To Margaret's way of thinking, Yoli likes to dilly-dally around too much in those bathrooms and in *her* part of the kitchen while Magda does her one-room number, then near the end of their shift, they reconnect to finish up the kitchen, the two of them together.

At home, at times, just for the hell of it, Margaret hits her husband smack in the gut with her fist. Shoves him. Slaps him, pulls his ears. Sometimes they wrestle to the floor where she pins him, pinches his nose and kisses him to pinpoint another win. He could whack her in return, knock the whey out of her, clearly in self defense. He could report her, but he wouldn't dream of hitting or reporting Garet. They have a fine time together.

Sarah Gerardi re-entered the house, adjusting her face mask. She owed it to Mother—or to humanity—to be cordial with the cleaning people. She would even issue them keys to the new locks. Behind her mask, Sarah fixed a smile on her lips. That's when she saw Stevie Calvert, also in a mask. They waved at each other, a bit too long.

Too many times. She wondered about Stevie. She played it through her mind: Here I go, fresh from showing Martin my poor body and all my scars last night, and he, dear old idiot, unlike me, he felt something, but not much, not enough; I was just as dead as he was, and we were both so relieved that it wasn't to be sex, but Marty, stupid man, no wit, he cried, tears for me, tears for us, for our mothers. He left before sunup, and now my perfidious heart is melting to see Stevie

Calvert's face. To yank his mask off. Please, somebody, call Cora Emerson, bring your big old gun. Come on over and just shoot me dead, Cora.

And all of us, these people working together, so oddly, everybody downstairs, are cleaning, fixing. Occasionally a workmen was heard hammering or starting up an electric drill. And Sarah wondered: Can they smell "cop" on me? They know about me, or do they? I don't have cop hair. Her hand fluffed her curls. But did she exude an aroma of Law-and-Order, did they hear in their heads the drumbeat and the news...*in Roeller County, as in Harris County, the criminal justice system's elite forensics unit led by Sarah Gerardi...*

Almost without exception, those working in the old homefront today shared Sarah's sense of unease. Everything seemed well-ordered, yet the atmosphere felt turbulent, silent. These were reticent people, shy. They needed an ice breaker, a dancer, maybe a striper—but in this town that would mean a furniture finisher. No, better if little children arrived singing Christmas carols, in March. *That* would warm them up. Or if a cute dog were to run through the place, a squirrel, a mouse. The very thought of mice in the house made Sarah conscious of a dizziness behind her eyes. It was unsettling. My eyes are going, and this place might explode, implode. She might explode. Or implode. She imagined herself folding down to nothingness, bye bye. I was once a cop-p-p, not no more.

Even the cleaning ladies seemed closed in and had changed-up their work routine. Instead of making a beeline to their preferred duty stations—big bathrooms, little bathroom, kitchen, long tall windows, dusty spots up high, baseboards—they stayed together in the open area Lynsey often called "the bowling alley."

Sarah saw Magda Guzman make a practice out of shining the dining table. She touched the spot where Lynsey's flowery laptop usually sat and asked Sarah, "*Miss, donde esta la computer laptop of Miss Lynsey?*"

Yoli looked up, as did Margaret. They glanced around the area. Yoli shrugged. Margaret mouthed the words, "Haven't seen it." Sarah told Magda, "*En la* repair shop." The women nodded. And Sarah frowned at herself, going insane, lying to this young woman: *I have lost it!*

Yoli gave Magda whispered instructions, something about the front door. Magda complied and wiggled in skin-tight tights toward the entrance hall. It was there she saw the marble floor, shiney and hard, besmeared with dark and wavy lines from yesterday's blood. Whoever had earlier tried a quick clean-up had left a worse sight. Probably the police. Magda spit it out, "*No respeto.*" The dancing, cleaning young mother held *no respeto* for cops, US or Mexican. "Right now," Magda told herself, "I smell cop." Moving closer to her aunt Yoli, she needed to warn her: Be careful. Pigs, *los cerdos*, pigs.

Five years ago, no matter all the talk, talk, talk today about the border, her crossing at Nuevo Laredo had been spooky, but not dangerous. For her, what hurt about leaving home were the names people called her, the way even her family thought she had been with a boy, not that a man on the bus had followed her. The pigs did nothing. Her mother slapped her. When it was obvious she was pregnant by that unknown rapist, her mother cried and wanted to hold Magda, to sit close with her. But her dad said little and would manage to leave or not enter a room where she was. One day her mother told her the plan. She would be crossing the border, going to live with her aunt, Tia Yoli and her dad's brother, Tio Sergio. But it is done now. Her aunt Yoli, and her uncle, and especially her cousins were dear to her now, and they all loved Aiden. For Magda, life was good.

And now there was the sound of a step stool and a ladder being dragged across bare floors. From the corner of her eye Magda saw a man standing outside on the veranda. He was looking around. Checking out the front entrance, getting closer to coming inside. "No," Magda muttered. A cop? In regular clothes. After the attack on Miss Lynsey, all the things stolen, the shooting, the killings out in the yard. The pigs will come and come again, asking questions, until they find a reason to take you to the jail. But people were greeting this guy—this old guy, a cop?—calling him Preston, *Preston.* Can it be that this giant pale old man is the son of Miss Lynsey? Maybe. Maybe not. Can't be. And behind him, a woman she knew she had never seen before, Anglo. Blonde. An ice blonde, bone-thin, she made Magda feel undressed, fat. Whoever these two are, they are *bizi bades. Los chismosos,* gossips. They want to start trouble.

"Excuse you," Magda warned the two strange interlopers. "Please. You two must stay out there." She carries a knife, a six-inch switchblade—too bad, it was in her purse in the storage room. The others were welcoming the man.

Magda turned her back to them and, peering down at the stripes of dried blood, Miss Lynsey's blood, felt she needed to touch the place, just to put her hand there, to protect Lynsey, her old friend.

Sarah went directly to her brother. How strange: She blurted out, "Where have you been?" Without answer, he spun around to introduce the blonde woman, the woman Preston had convinced himself in less than 24-hours was his soulmate, his lifeline, his fiancée-to-be. And she, the blonde, Cinnah Shelton of Cal-Tex News & Mysteries, confused and a bit bemused, told herself: Whatever this is, just let it play itself out. *Que sera, sera.* It's been less than a day, but whatever will be, it will be.

As Magda placed her hand on the cool dried blood, she felt weak, dizzy. Squatting, she bowed her head. For her, there was a deeper loss with Lynsey gone. *"No pertenezo."* "I don't belong," in English. No longer, never again, to be part of Lynsey, this house. After all that had already been transient in her life, never before had Magda said it, but she did now: *"Estoy perdida."* "I am lost." Aware that a good person would soon die, and her dry blood was right here, Magda swayed. Free of self-control, of restrictions, she cried out in her mother tongue what was in her heart, *"Miss Lynsey. Oh, que triste. La sangre de Señora Lynsey. Tia, su sangre de ayer, como la podemos laver?"*

The girl fell dramatically to the floor.

Sarah immediately felt the translation, and softly repeated Magda's words: "'Miss Lynsey. Oh, so sad... the blood of Mrs. Lynsey...it's her blood from yesterday. How can we—or who can—wash it away?"

Sarah and Yoli together gathered Magda up into their arms and guided her to a sofa. Sarah darted toward the kitchen and grabbed a bottle of cold water for the girl, and a dish towel. Then, face to face with her brother, Sarah put her hand flat on his chest. She said, "Magda is very upset. Did you 'get' all that she said?"

Preston, the brother, answered, "I was speaking Spanish when you were still crying, 'Ma-ma, wa-wa.'"

"I think not. You couldn't even speak English. Mother says you never spoke a word until you were five, and I arrived."

"Maybe," he said, "everything was Ok until then."

"What? With two bigger brothers pounding on you. Hollis and Yuri. Go ahead, say they never pounded you."

"Not as I recall."

"You and Mother live in a dreamworld," Sarah said.

"And you live in a nightmare. What were you doing, after *last* night, you told me on the phone, stayin' with Marty, now you're over there muggin' up to Stevie Calvert?"

Sarah shot back. "What are you doing with Cinnamon Bun?" Preston frowned, but stopped. There was a lot he could sling at his sister about a lot of things. But not now. He said, "Do you want to drive me, and you, to the hospital after this?"

"Ok, I will pick you up at the office. We need to see Faust about Mother's laptop."

"I have it. He gave it to me this morning. It's in my car."

Sarah calculated the matters at hand. Preston deserved a fist in the snout, on general purposes, but not today.

She leaned closer, pulled her mask down, and whispered in the general vicinity of his ear, "Listen, Magda really cares. About Mother. She asks how we will clean the blood. So, damn it. Preston, *do* something."

"I'll do it," he said, taking control, throwing off his jacket. "Thank you, Madga. If someone will give me a cloth and water, I'll wash away my mother's blood. Right now."

"No, I will," Sarah said, "or we can do it together. Maybe Magda..."

Yoli, leader of Squad Two, spoke up, "We can do it. It is our job, Miss. Mr. Preston. All of Squad Two. We have been her team and we will all do it. Ok?"

"Mr. Gerardi," Max Crawford, well-known carpenter in San Mateo, called out, "may I suggest that everybody here—we all know Lynsey. Let everyone here—that wants to—we each take a turn. If someone can't, that is Ok, but we will fix this house and clean it so when she comes in that door, over there, every single thing is just so. Sir? What do you say."

Preston nodded. "Please let me say thanks to all of you. I was at the trauma hospital last night, with Cinnah Shelton, who kindly drove me there."

Sarah said to herself: "Preston. Stop talking. '...kindly *drove* me there...' and then kindly drove you to what? The no-tell mo-tel on the highway?"

Preston was saying, about the military trauma hospital, "It is a large, very serious place. I could see only a little through some glass partitions, but they must have had ten doctors around my mother, discussing every aspect of her, well, you know, her situation. And while we could not go inside the ER, to see her, Lynsey, they told us, she had gotten blood, oxygen and liquids. She had four fractured ribs and a deflated lung. They are draining her chest, so that she doesn't get pneumonia. For now, they'll wait to see about her shoulder. Shoulders can be tricky, right? Some of you know."

Sarah was frowning: "Shut up, shut the hell up."

Preston continued his presentation. "Probably this morning they will have finished surgery on her jaw, her face, where he hit her with a wrench. They are watching her kidneys, where she apparently was kicked several times when she was down, over there, right where the blood, and yes, maybe where urine stains may be. Also, for now, she has been placed in an induced coma, so her body can rest up, maybe heal. Believe me, they, the army doctors, medics, are doing their best. And right now, they say she will be at SAMMC for a while and then at another facility, in rehab, recovery." He paused.

A male voice shouted in a thin echoey voice, "We all are prayin' she recovers, and comes home soon."

Preston spoke, louder than before, "Thank you all so much. I hope she can come to San Mateo for rehab. We'll let you guys, and ladies, know, as soon as we do. Thank you all, especially for prayers."

'Well, people," it was Max Crawford again, "let's get on with this floor. We'll take care of it for Lynsey."

And then, down on his knees, Preston took the old soft towel that he recognized briefly, a pan of water, offered to him by Yoli. She handed him a bottle of Mr. Shine & Clean, a roll of paper towels, and a kitchen knife. He was the first, this day, to work at cleaning away the remnants of his mother's attack.

Sarah, as if this were normal, chatted with Cinnah, and waited for her brother so that she could be next. They switched places. Then Sarah switched with Yoli. No one made an effort to do all the cleaning himself, herself, but turned the job over to the next one. Before long, it was finished, the wiping, the chipping away of the long stained patch of dried blood and smears.

The downstairs people turned back to their individual chores, their skills, yet they seemed to regard the place where Lynsey had lain as the centerpoint of their attention. Some had ignored the blood cleaners as they worked. Others kept watch, even after taking a turn. They were strangely satisfied. They were becoming a band, a gang, secret daredevils in the time of COVID, in the fight against crime. There also happened to be blood stains outside near the sidewalk. And on the dry grass. They would get all that washed away as well.

Sarah wanted to ask Cinnah, the only reasonable outsider available, possibly a clear thinker, "Are we crazy? Carrying on too much about the stains? I mean, it's not like the blood of Jesus or anything." But her mother had taught her well. You don't involve strangers. It might embarrass them. Sarah said not a word to the blonde woman, just began texting on her phone.

And then, down in a squat, where she had been scrubbing strange spots on the carpet, Margaret Conant sat up. Giving her ponytail a shake, she popped her collar so it was up, and maskless, broke the silence with a song:

"Were you there when they crucified my Lord? Were you there when they crucified my Lord?"

(Author's note: For online readers, several links to music videos appear in this chapter. Tap the link, try to hit the blue *youtube*—then choose "Full Screen," click off any advertisements that may have broken through our security, and enjoy a few minutes of the same music the book's characters are hearing. To return to reading, just reverse the steps. For paper readers, the link and the information line can direct you to where you may find the song, or dance, on YouTube.)

https://youtu.be/LRaFdFkOVyY.

(*YouTube:* Pegasus, "Were You There?")

"Were you there when they nailed him to the tree? Were you there when they nailed him to the tree? Were you there when they laid him in the tomb?"

The workers, fourteen in number, were dazed, shocked, some perhaps were lost in memories, in guilt, in embarrassment, but the song was good. The girl could sing. A real sweet girl to dare that. Some tried to hide tears. Sarah Gerardi made silent clapping hands and said in a loud whisper behind her mask, "Well done, Garet. Very well done."

Like an airy cloud changing shape, soon a tiny patch of time drifted away and the fourteen mortals—from San Mateo and not from San Mateo—working downstairs, or texting on a cell phone, were mostly silent. On their own, they ignored each other, until a booming newcomer sashayed in through the open doorway with a clutter of fashionable canvas grocery bags lined up on her arms and clutching one large shining insulated bag to her chest. A cheerful corn-fed woman, she shouted, "Hi, everyone. I could hear the singing when I just opened my car door. Was it Garet? Yeah, I thought so. She's my girl." A few of the sturdy fourteen looked baffled. Her girl?

"Oh, hey, sorry, y'all, my name is JoJo Certuche. I'm Miss Gerardi's food service person, her grocery shopper, and her chef. The family cook. Preston, Sarah. Hiya, howdy. I'll just unpack more in the car. Then be doin' my thing in the kitchen. Hello, Magda, Miz Yoli, how're y'all? And my buddy Margaret. Hi, sugar. Hey, can Garet *sing*, or what? Hello, all you fellows, here and there, Mr. Crawford, Mr. Calvert, all you guys, hello. Anybody want to help me with the food?" And Jason Cosby, only 19, and Max Crawford's squirrelly carpenter apprentice, jumped up from what he was doing. "I love food. I volunteer." He was on it.

JoJo reminded him to change gloves. Then she winked widely at Preston. And smiled questioningly at Cinnah.

Preston, tagging Cinnah along with him, made the rounds speaking with the ten or twelve others, saying hello and thanks, while JoJo and Jason Cosby were in the kitchen, making small noises. Soon a man's voice rose higher, lighter, than a buzz. Max Crawford. He was humming, and then singing his song, a hard one to carry, but today he figured he had a room filled with silent singers, brothers and sisters, hummers to help him to the end. From the beginning, Max sang:

https://youtu.be/dZ1jQJDPQhg.
(YouTube: Matt Nichol, "Amazing Grace")

"Amazing Grace, how sweet the sound That saved a wretch like me.

I once was lost but now am found Was blind but now I see—"

Everyone knew this was Max's true-blue serenade, a sacred ceremony, almost. Max, an-old time carpenter, a San Mateo handyman, artesian, popular with homeowners and builders, was the man at today's center. "Thank you, Max," people told him. "Thanks for that song." "Very nice." "Always makes me cry." "Very nice, sir."

Max sniffed and wiped at one eye. "It's true," he said. Well over sixty, he was still hanging sheet rock for a living, climbing on rooftops, although those jobs took more control than he sometimes had available. He said, "Ask my wife. I was lost, and now I'm, just doin' a whole lot better."

A sigh, a gasp, went around Lynsey's "bowling alley" living-dining room. Some clapped. Max Crawford, like Lynsey's first cousin Silvia Ann, had skin cancer. Silvia died early. And these people and families, the Crawfords, the Calverts, Al Koett's family, the Guzman family, the Cosby family, the Guerras, the Gerardi family, JoJo and her family, they all lived in a town where almost everybody knew everybody else, families, couples and singles. They had gone through school together, worked side-by-side, lived peacefully as neighbors, inter-married, were friendly, not friendly, and were well kept-up on the affairs—real or imagined—the doings, and the health of the others. Some people in San Mateo could be up to date on some person's health or marital status and yet not recognize the person if face-to-face. Most of them knew Max to be a survivor of Cutaneous T-Cell Lymphoma. Called CTCL, the condition is not exactly skin cancer but blood cancer. Every person has T-cells, in great numbers on the skin. T-cells prevent infections, but sometimes what seems like a rash, or the heartbreak of psoriasis, is actually one of the two types of CTCL. Max has mycosis fungoides, the most common, but slower to develop, type.

Still, he gets up every morning, ready for work, these days preferring small jobs, quickly finished. With no son or son-in-law interested in his carpentry business, Max watches each new employee. Of his two workers today, he knows Jason Cosby is out of the picture, but Max has high hopes for Dave Guerra, a really steady worker, had building experience from a couple tours with the army combat construction engineers; Preston's guys, you might say. Max could have turned this job today over to Dave, were it not for the Gerardi family. Everyone knew it, none would say it, but under threat of COVID, Max should be at home. With social distancing next to impossible, the workers depend on masks and gloves. They try.

After the singing of Amazing Grace, their minds likely checking memory banks for enough words to get through the chorus of their own favorite, the dozen-plus were silent. For hard working adults, the thought of public singing is a natural cause of faintheartedness. Others thought, what the heck, somebody will know it. This is my gang. Today. They'll help me. Someone will pick it up.

"Here's one." Stevie from Calvert's Locksmith, nephew of the original Mr. Calvert, now owner of three locksmith businesses in two counties, one about to close now with people staying home, not spending on locks—and Sarah Gerardi's erstwhile dance partner from that rained-out night during her sophomore year—shouted out from a wide tall window where he was installing new hardware. "Y'all? Ready for this one?"

From above them, he began in a trusty voice: *"Mine eyes have seen the glory of the coming of the Lord…"*

https://youtu.be/irshiU70SnA.

(*YouTube:* Charlie Szabo, "The Battle Hymn of the Republic")

His participating audience of a dozen or so clapped, agreed, "Great song."

After a bit, Magdalena stood. Without introduction, she began slowly singing *"Panis Angelicus,"* a hymn in Latin.

Often, people familiar with the song prefer it in Latin, like to forget the English, as a way to simply surrender to the sounds. Some like to sing in their own made-up words, a phenomenon, some say, not unlike singing or praying in tongues. When Magda, singer now as well as salsa dancer, kept on with her song, even those who had not heard it before were mesmerized and hummed along:

https://youtu.be/MY7s2yiVpIo.

(*YouTube:* Barlowgirl, "Panis Angelicus")

Panis angelicus, fit panis hominum, dat panis coelicus

The angel's bread, bread of men, the heavenly bread

Figuris terminum, O res mirablis, Manducat dominum...

Ends all symbols, Oh, miraculous thing! The Lord's body..."

At the end of the clapping, Sarah leaned toward Preston and Cinnah to show off a bit, "The original words were written by Thomas Aquinas, in the 13th century."

Preston couldn't resist. "Didn't he have an illegitimate child and lots of hooker gal friends?"

"What are you tryin' to tell us, Preston?" Sarah snapped.

"No, y'all," Cinnah kicked in, "Preston's talking about Saint Augustine, doctor of the church. He had a child, he'd been a playboy, but his mother, Saint Monica, had prayed for him, for ages, years. He offered marriage, but no. The girl went to a convent where she died, and the little boy, baptized the same day as Augustine, died as well."

"Stories. Bits of gossip," Sarah mouthed thoughtfully—when what she wanted to do was shout, "Wow, blondy-blonde, gimme *fi*, you are a super Catholic!"

"And you know this *history*, how?" Preston asked his future fiancée-to-be-to-be, surprising his sister who, as usual, suspected Preston was pretending with the blonde bun that he was a sweet kind guy, never hateful.

"It's *church* history," Cinnah shot back, a second surprise to Sarah who expected Miss Blondie to kowtow to old Preston, her hot new (old) guy of the hour.

"Storytellers," Sarah insisted. "Before pen and ink, they passed along the info, and the gossip, we call history."

"They probably wish they had lived here in San Mateo instead of some backwater village in Italy where today the number of coronavirus deaths may even exceed that recorded in China," Preston told them, gaining steam, even while having made some kind of puzzling statement.

Cinnah stood up to him. "Seven thousand people have died of the pandemic, in Italy, as of *today*, Preston."

"Three thousand have died in Northern Spain," Sarah told him. "In *Spain*, where Jewel, and Rose—"

Cinnah said, "*Oh!* That's your—*hm*, like you say. So sad. And now. Nearly 700 deaths in the U.S. It's unreal."

The alarm system guy, new to San Mateo, stood then, apart from his work, and spoke in a deep voice, "My name is Dor Barish, hello, I'm from Israel, born in Jerusalem. I am here in Texas, working, for eight months now. I have my son and wife here, and a brother also. May I tell you, y'all, when I was three years old and my brother—was an infant—my mother died, and my father and I and the baby moved in with his parents. Sometimes it happens, but my father became like a big brother to us. My *grandmother*, really, brought us up. She will soon be 95, but because of COVID, now we can't go back home, even to visit. Anyhow, sorry. It is what it is. I don't know Mrs. Gerardi, but my grandmother would sometimes shake a her finger at the cabbage heads watching from the window, the gossips—we call them—"

Someone shouted, "The *yenta tele bentas*"—and Magda called out, "They are called *bizi bades* and Miz Lynsey does not like them."

Dor smiled and nodded. "You know one gossip, you know them all. And I see Mrs. Gerardi and my grandmother would be chums, like peas in a pod. Imagine how they would *kvetch* about all the *bizi bades* on this planet. Perhaps they will, over Facebook. Or Instagram. Aristotle said a friend is one single soul dwelling in two bodies. And those two, someday, they may be friends like that. My grandmother, dear lady, her name is Naomi, the mother-in-law of Ruth—I always imagine them grubbing in the field for leftover grain—we called my bobe *Mi*. When I was a boy, Mi sent me out for elocution lessons. I practiced with the old fashioned tape recorder—I was more interested in the tape machine than in speaking, but my *bobe* would go over every word, in Hebrew and in English, with me. Perhaps she thought I would grow up to be the new H.V. Kaltenborn, the famous radio commentator.

"Do you know it?" he asked. "The story of the royal family of Potato land? Not Poland, Potato Land. Ah, may I tell it to you? Ok, the king and queen had three daughters. One day, they were sitting around eating curly fries, when the oldest daughter announced, 'I am getting married.' The mother is very happy and says, '*Mazel Tov*, what a wedding we will have. Oh, and who is the groom?'

"'I am marrying Ron Russet.'"

"'A Russet! Oh, Russets, such fine taters. Great family line, a distant cousin, but no worries. We must start planning the wedding. You will be a beautiful bride.'

"Not to be out done—and this is for my partner over there, Jeb McMichael, say hello to Jeb, he's an Irishman—the second daughter announces to the family, 'I also will be having a wedding, very soon,' and her parents say, 'We noticed a bump, but who will marry you? Like *this?*' The second daughter, always a wild one, answers, 'Well, forgive me, but the truth is, I am already married, and expecting potatoes of my own, see?' And she held up her vine of Lucky Charm cereal pieces hung around her neck.

"The head of Potato Land asked his daughter, 'And so who does this? Who supplies you, a simple girl, just a small potato, with Lucky Charms on a vine?'

Some of Dar's listeners looked confused. He continued, "Second daughter, oblivious to her father's skepticism, was bubbling, and blushing with pure joy. She said, 'He is an *Irish* tater. They call him Pat the Potato.'

"'Oh.' The head of all potatoes mused, 'Ok. Lovely. Among potato heads everywhere, Irish taters are famous, fabulous. Have royal roots. Some of them.'

"Well now," Dar Barish from Jerusalem said, continuing his potato tale. "The youngest daughter, still a student at Potato University, stood and said, 'Mum, Dad, I also am a bride to be—' and her mother cried out, 'But you are too young.'

And the king shouted out, 'Who dares propose marriage to my tiny princess, number three? What is his name?' And she tells her parents, 'It will be fine. He is wealthy, and famous—'

"The king yells, 'His name! *Now!'*

"The tater tot said softly, 'Abba, please, listen, I am not marrying a legume or some silly sweet potato, I have been proposed to by a widely admired American radio speaker and, if you must know, his name is Hans von Kaltenborn— that's H.V. Kaltenborn, and Hans says—'

"'No. Never!' The royal potatoes were steaming, hot.

"The older sister-spuds stood trembling. They had never seen their parents so upset and now the crusty old king of all potatoes in the land was shouting at his baby potato, 'You are a royal tater, you can never marry H.V. Kaltenborn, or Dan Rather, or Rush Limbaugh—'

"'But why?' she cried out, 'why?'

"'Because those spuds, Kaltenborn, Limbaugh, Dan Rather, no matter how you prepare them, sliced, diced, creamed, fried, baked—they are *common taters.'*

"A long way to show you that, while I can not sing as these others, so beautiful—but for my grandmother Naomi, and for Lynsey, I can *speak.* I can not sing, although I have a young son who puts Hebrew songs to rap. Perhaps *he* can not sing. If you permit, I will do my best. Perhaps you know it, Psalm 27. If I can remember the words, the very words we need to hear during this pandemic: Be strong, and let your heart take courage: Wait upon the Lord, ladies and gentlemen.

https://youtu.be/_UcqBZAeaFY.
(*YouTube:* Ted Hildebrant, "Psalm 27")

"And in English, Psalm 27, you may recognize the words: *'The Lord is my light and my salvation: do I fear? The Lord is my life's refuge; of whom am I afraid? When evildoers come at me to devour my flesh, These enemies and foes themselves stumble and fall. Though armies encamp around me, I fear not…'"*

While Margaret made a dash to the kitchen to see JoJo, the serious Christians, anxious to ask Dor about Jerusalem, eager to praise his voice, gathered around him, at six feet distances. Those remaining, with a job yet to complete, got back to business, but soon JoJo came out of the kitchen and called everyone to follow her, more or less, into the kitchen, to the kitchen table. "It's time to eat, a little snack—just soup and sandwiches, and some yummy extras, but we know Miz Lynsey would love to have you in her kitchen. Even at distances. You'll see. And after that, we have a special cake and chocolate almond cookies on the big table, cake and cookies made by yours truly, and Jason will be serving Blue Bell ice cream, Homemade Vanilla and Mint Chocolate Chip, or both together, if ya like it that way, out on the veranda. All disposable bowls and plates, cups, and utensils, so don't worry. We'll pass around hand sanitizers and trash bags. Please, come. And If you feel crowded, and worry about social distance, remember you are welcome to sit out back on the porch. Or anywhere there's a bench, or, uh, a chair. There's even a swing in Miz Lynsey's backyard.What? Oh, you say Jason was tryin' out the swing this morning. Why not? I'm not surprised. Now, at arm's length. Very long arms."

She gestured to Preston, apparent boss of the Gerardi clan, "Mr. Preston, Sarah. Magda, come on, *eat*, Garet—hey, y'all, we went to high school together, *yaaay*, high school, the worst-best time of your life. Now. Everyone. To the kitchen. Now. Things may be melting."

After a while, Jeb McMichael stood up. He's the spare, skinny wizzkid who is currently in business with Dor Barish. Jeb, who had been silent most of the morning, seems a good-hearted bloke. He had been a drinker, but everybody knew that. Now, standing by the entrance to the kitchen, he announced in a booming, but stressed, voice, "Thank you for the meal. My friends. I can't do much to comfort the family after the terrible event that happened here, but Dor and I are going to fix this place up to the highest tech standards possible at this time. Right now, I'd like to sing the song that Irish outlaws love most. But first, I need you to know the story. Danny—yes, our Danny boy was an emigrant, gone from home. Legal. Or maybe not, but he was in exile. Of some sort, somewhere. Yes! I hear you. *You know him*. You know the song. *What?*

"One minute. Dar is crying over there for me to get on with it. He talked longer than me. He's the one with hyperactivity, not me. The man talks my ear off. In the truck, I am like, 'Shut up, man,' but he's my boss. Anyhow, some people say, *Danny Boy* is a guilt trip. I mean, if it's about a father calling out to his adult son, sort of threatenin' him that when the guy finally comes back home, the dad will be long dead, is that a guilt trip? I say no. You have to know the Irish and their history. I invite, I beg ya—a quick lesson. Look up and listen to just one song. It's called "Flight of Earls." *Flight of Earls*, written by a fella called Reilly, way back in the 1980s, it's about the jet flights that leave Dublin Airport, carrying *now* well-educated youngsters, leaving Ireland because there's no jobs at home, but you know what? These days those same airplanes—they fly both ways—they will bring the kids, no matter their age, back home to Ireland, to visit or back to stay. Dor and I talk about this all the time. Or he does. Leaving your home country, especially in times of trouble, man, it's tough. It makes you sick with sadness and worry. So this song is for everyone, for the family—they tell me Lynsey's mother was Irish. Irish-American. Her mother was born here. It takes more than one generation to heal over, but, well, moving on, some say the song is about gay lovers. Or a mother and son. Nope. It's a call to Danny, a son who may be walking 'the streets of Baltimore' right this minute as Liam Reilly tells us in 'Flight of the Earls,' or Danny may be one of the "Leaders of the future...far away from home..." And there's a pretty lady here today, a member of our group, and *she's a Danny*. Miss Magda, give her a hand. What a voice. Anyhow, sing with me. I'd do this a whole lot better if I had a drink in my hand, but don't tell my sponsor. Anyhow, 'Danny' is essentially a plea to all the crazy and rambling Dannys of the world, in all countries, from any country. And it's always the same: Come home, you will be welcome, and that's not likely to change:

"Oh, Danny boy, the pipes, the pipes are calling From glen to glen, and down the mountain side.

https://youtu.be/xlzWRQ5e4qg.
(*YouTube:* Finbar Wright, "Danny Boy")

The summer's gone, and all the roses falling, It's you, it's you must go and I must bide.

But come ye back when summer's in the meadow, Or when the valley's hushed and white with snow, It's I'll be here in sunshine or in shadow,

Oh, Danny boy, oh Danny boy, I love you so."

Shortly, on that Thursday morning, a day after Lynsey's attack, JoJo and Margaret—Garet—stood together, but apart in the window that opened to the veranda. "Y'all," JoJo shouted. "Don't know about you, but any more sad songs and I'm going to need that drink Jeb mentioned. So Garet, mostly Garet, and I have a little pick-me-up ditty. The first two lines may be all we remember, but we are going to do an oldie we used to sing and groove to back in choir class. It's called 'Glow Worm.' Join us, maybe kick up your heels, twist a little. Do the jitterbug. And I think Miz Lynsey would approve of *that*, don't you? A little jitterbug. Ok, Garet, hit it:"

"Shine little glow-worm, glimmer glimmer! Shine, little glow-worm, glimmer, glimmer!"

https://youtu.be/ciytVmA5QWQ. (*YouTube:* Bill Kline, "Glow Worm"

Magda and Dave Guerra, prime apprentice to Max Crawford, who had been talking during lunch, did a few salsa steps to Glow Worm and earned some cheers. Others, music finished, work finished, were slipping away. The morning had been *almost* too intense. Too much closeness. Never to be repeated. Like graduation night. *Sad*. It wasn't even noon and Sarah was exhausted, worn out. She could not believe it, all this carrying-on. In harmony with her laziness, she took the elevator, not the stairs that nagged her, "Ok, get fat, and die." In her room, next door to the room she had shared with Jewel, she threw herself on her bed, and moaned, "I am *done*..."

Unable to rest, she reached for her laptop and began writing—what else—a journal entry, in a format that seemed so natural to her.

ONE, SARAH MADDY'S FIRST ADULT JOURNAL

March 26, 2020 SAN MATEO, TEXAS

Mother, how did it happen? You're in the trauma hospital, with soldiers, and retirees, and in less than 24 hours Preston has found the woman of his dreams. Preston has a girlfriend! The first in a million years.

Even weirder, she is nice, seem 90 percent normal, and it looks as if she likes him. Today they were almost holding hands, glued to each other. This is not the horrible selfish grouchy old Preston we know who moves away from women, moves away from everybody, but all of them think he is so damn great. I may be crazy but I welcome her. Whatever we think is seriously wrong with her (and there has to be something) I hope they get married and find great happiness.

But I'm not giving up my suite of rooms.

What's the time?

I wonder if Romeo pants still thinks I am driving him. To see about you. Anyhow, before I forget, I wanted to tell you. I better just go, but first, I know you will never read this because I alone, of everybody, I am the one to realize you will not be coming home. But you must know that nobody, but nobody, ever had a better accidental farewell or more spontaneous last rites than you today.

Songs, fun and sad. We heard 'Danny Boy,' and some people cried, some of us. You remember when we went to Ireland? You were so excited and I was such a brat. What can I say? Sorry. JoJo had this helper. I think his name was Jason Cosby—working for Max Crawford. Graduated HS in 2019. And he did a break dance on the back porch. Really masculine, like Rocky, if Rocky were made out of rubber, or silly glue. The kid, Jeb or Jason. No, I think it's Jason—yes, Jason gave a sweet thanks to Max. In June he has a date with the Marines. OORAH! Danny Boy, USA. Don't cry. They might send him home. Break dancer, and all.

Come home. We need to talk. I sort of slept with Martin last night and then almost literally—shall we decide not to debate "almost literally"?—threw myself at Stevie Calvert today, but all he could do was peel me off of himself and introduce me to his assistant, guy named Al Koett. Wasn't there an Al Koett, about 15 years younger than me, in prison for robbing the check-cashing place out on Eye 35? Beat up a woman at Serita's beer joint? Now he's workin' as a locksmith. Help.

Came creepin' around later, wanting to know if I'd like to come over for dranks since the bars are closed. Surprised he didn't ask me to brang the dranks.

Oh, Mother! Is this what I have become? At 56? Passed-around passed-over? What's the joke? Ok. Why is Sarah like the heel in a loaf of bread? Because everybody's touched her and nobody wants her. Hell, I never could tell a joke. Or you either. We're not fun people.

Also, I still have someone on the string in Houston. A single guy. Don't start on me.

Oh, and Preston's future wife, the one he met yesterday, she has a little boy, Kevin. He's eight. She's Catholic, divorced, annulled. So, yay. Ready to roll. Yes, I know Martin is Catholic, but he's not my type. Anyhow, old Pres. He might marry the girl, but he'll never leave his mother. And I am really sorry about Ireland. Over & out, Sarah Madd~

Chapter ten ~ the Funeral

"Stone walls do not a prison make"

To Althea, from Prison

-Richard Lovelace

The late Cesar Caraman didn't have much in the way of family in Roeller County. A mother, an aunt and uncle, a couple of distant cousins. He had grown up in California, playing wide receiver for his middle school and high school football teams. Until one night he jumped up to catch a ball and came down hard at an awkward angle, tearing up one knee. When a boatload of painkillers and one surgery late in his senior year and a follow-up surgery early the next year didn't seem to help, Caraman turned to a gym well-known for offering an alphabet of vitamins, supplements, and steroids. When that didn't help, he again turned to prescribed painkillers, to opioid drugs, to oxycontin. Then, frustrated by the federal cutback on prescription drugs, he began ro track any narcotic available, legal or illegal.

His pattern was to work steadily at punishing, tediously monotonous manual labor—construction, roadwork, moving furniture, loading and unloading heavy equipment, demolishing old buildings, general landscaping, even at times cleaning offices and homes.

And when his few debts were paid and with adequate cash in the bank, he'd quit work and binge on his soon dwindling collection of legal stuff, Narco, Oxy. Lots of weed, until all gone. See? Gone-gone, then he'd rip into his more challenging collection of street drugs, or any mind-numbing or hypnotic substance he could lay his hands upon. Then, he'd try the Emergency Room, crying and sniveling from intense back pain, get a collection of whatever he could, and start again. In short, he was a junkie, an intentional and deliberate but largely self-funded junkie. Home robbery and assault on the elderly was, apparently, a new gig for him.

The night of his funeral service, Cesar's family had a box of surgical masks and a box of gloves to offer to the reporters they had invited from local television and radio stations, from every Mid-Texas newspaper, even the weeklies, as well as some bloggers and podcasters recommended by Cesar's cousin, Shelby Blancas, a geek who held an associate degree in social studies from the local community college. Cousin Shelby ran a guitar store, recognized at its core by the two-dozen member Roeller County underground drug defense group as "Yaqub's Weed Shop." Fortunately, or unfortunately, only three such reporters showed up, and one other fellow dressed in a charcoal suit, tie bar gleaming with the tiny initials of his unremarkable law school, who recorded the action on his cell phone, everything that was said that evening. Then there were Cesar's three twentyish cousins, and one tall older pale man who stood in the street next to a sporty Chevy Equinox, yet it all worked out well enough. The family, attentive to the dangers of COVID-19 and aware of the need for social distancing, had, besides the gloves and masks, brought out white plastic chairs, an old rocker from the backyard, and several camp stools. With great care, they had them positioned, a dozen seats in two semicircles, each at least six feet, or so, from the other.

The three reporters, along with Cesar's three cousins, and the young man in a suit all sat facing the mother, aunt, and uncle who sat ground level at a bare table in front of a high front porch and therefore exactly in front of and *under* a porch table which was covered in a Dallas Cowboys blanket. A mid-size spotlight, swaying in the breeze, glared down on Cesar's glossy white ceramic urn placed in the center of the Cowboy blanket or, alternately, the small spotlight shone directly into the eyes of the reporters, the man in a suit, the three cousins, and the pale white man. At the stroke of seven, on a cool Wednesday, April Fool's Day, 2020, Cesar's funeral began with his mother standing to speak first.

"Thank you, everyone, for coming out tonight to remember my son's life during this coronavirus. And for wearing the masks and gloves. I am not wearing *no* mask at all right now because I have to talk, and I am nervous, and ashamed. I'm Gloria, I'm Cesar's mom. This is my brother, Tony, and his wife, Andrea. We are all named Caraman. Well, we just want to give glory to God for my son's life, for the years we had him with us."

Gloria moved closer to the reporters and others. She said, "Excuse me, I won't come no closer but I want you to hear me. My voice has been bothering me. I have been crying so much, all of us, just crying and crying. Well, you all know, my son was in California. And I was here. I told him it's nice out here. There is always work, from the building on the highway. So, he came to us, here in San Mateo, three years ago. I can't say it was the right or the wrong thing, with what all has happened now." Cesar's mother covered her face with her hands. Her brother and sister-in-law stared at her as if she were a total stranger.

She cried out in surprise, "Oh! We're not supposed to touch our face, sorry." Her sister-in-law passed her a small clutch of tissues. "Well, I don't want to waste your time. I will tell you, as far as Cesar was concerned, California is a bad place. He got into trouble, the *first* time"—Tony and Andrea Caraman nodded in assent, yeah, that first time was *bad*—"after his girlfriend over there in California brought 'domestic battery' charges against him. What is that, 'domestic battery'?"

Mr. Tony Caraman stood, ready to answer, "They make a charge of domestic violence and that don't even require a visible injury. You can just tell 'em, 'He hit me, he choke me.' And what is it?" Tony asked the reporters and cousins, and the young man in a suit who had a smirk on his face, the cell tight in his hand, but who had now arranged himself into a comfortable man-sprawl: good thing the family utilized social distancing. Cesar's uncle answered his own question. "It is good for women pushed around and beaten, bruised faces, broken arms, sometimes for decades. Not so good for big guys, young, who have wives or girlfriends out to revenge for the *possibility* they have been pushed around, for however long. And that's all I've got to say. Except we all know that Cesar Antonio Caraman was a big guy, six-two, 225 to 240 pounds. He was 18, 19, at that time. Now. Let her talk. She's the mother. I don't care."

The mother continued to explain that young Caraman, still in his early 20s, relocated, legally, to Texas and either rebuilt his life or continued his downward path, but then he went back. Back to California, and came back. All seemed Ok, until that March day, 2020, when not the COVID virus, but a bullet caught him in the back of the head, and killed him. "March 25th," she explained.

His mother, a large dark-haired, dark-eyed woman in her forties, but appearing to be in her fifties, again moved herself closer to her guests. "Excuse me, my voice. Well, Cesar took his punishment"—a gasp rose up to meet the evening air— "over there in California, 18 months, then they turned it into just *six* months in jail, and a year probation, all because that bitch lied about him. He came to Texas legally, no problem, but he couldn't get no decent job, just bits and pieces, because of what happened in California, but he was trying and trying just to build up his life. He'd say, 'Mommy, I am going to turn my life around.' He told me, 'You will be proud of me.'"

Her sister-in-law clearly held to the belief that Cesar had joined them in Texas to build up his life. "He was *turning* his life around," the aunt of Cesar Caraman called out while his uncle sulked in silent disgust.

Money was tight for the small family, even more so now after Cesar's mom had lost her job at The Drinking Spot Bar & Taco Shop, which closed earlier in March in the fight against COVID-19. And then, now, even though funerals of no more than ten at a time were postponed indefinitely, there remained certain end-of-life expenses.

"They *make* you pay," Tia Andrea began in a strong voice, while still seated at the table on the grass, but Gloria, as was her place as Cesar's mom, brightened up to explain the situation in detail, "Y'all need to know, I haven't had no work in three weeks. They just lock the doors, and put up a big sign, CLOSED. And, at the funeral home, they put you in a room, round a table, and they go one by one, asking, 'How much can you pay? Next, how much can you pay? Do you have a credit card? Do you have some relatives to call? How much can they pay?' Over and over. You can't leave. And they just keep at it until they come up with the money."

For this reason, the Caraman family had decided on cremation and an outdoor service on their family porch. Also, they did not want to expose anyone to that virus.

"We will take your questions now," Gloria announced.

The reporters, one or two of the three of them, were shielding their eyes from the glare of the funeral spotlight. They seemed, even from a distance of six feet, to mumble with each other in reporter code. One asked Gloria, the mother, in a modified tone, "Yes, I was wondering. How did the two men meet?"

Gloria looked bewildered, "What two men?" she asked.

The reporter spoke up, "How did your son Cesar meet Noe Alejandro? The man who was shot along with your son? After they, ah, broke into Lynsey Gerardi's house?"

"I don't know. In the gym," she said. "I never heard of that guy until after *m'ijo* came from California."

"Excuse me," the same reporter asked, "you mean your son was more recently in California?"

"Tony, when was that he got back?"

Tony Caraman calculated. "He left here on Sunday, March first, that was in 2020, and he came back on the 16th, I think it was a Monday. Yes, Monday, the 16th."

The reporters were tapping this information into their tablets, their cell phones. And then one shouted out, "Excuse me, so Cesar went *back* to California in December 2019, then returned to Texas but went again *back* to California on March the first, returning again to San Mateo on March the 16th?"

"Yes," the family members agreed. "That's right."

"Do you recall when, what date, was it when Cesar came back to San Mateo, after Christmas 2019?"

Cesar's mother, troubled, closed her eyes. "Ooo. It was January. We had summer weather. I'll say January, the 16th. He complained how hot it was here, y'know?"

A male reporter, the older one, called out, "What were Cesar's talents and ambitions. What did he want to do with his life? How did he like to spend his free time?"

Gloria, Andrea, and Tony consulted each other. "Police Officer," Gloria shouted. "He wanted to be a police officer." She shrugged. "Or a deputy sheriff!" Good answer. Tony and Andea nodded in agreement. "Police officer, or deputy sheriff."

Tony Caraman let out a vicious laugh, "Cesar didn't have no 'free time.' He was always on the hunt."

The reporter who had not yet asked a question, squinted into the spotlight and, ignoring Tony's "the hunt" comment, heard herself ask the family, "Why would Cesar beat an elderly woman; she was 87. Why hit her with a pipe wrench, kick her, almost to death?"

Gloria's voice became louder, but she was sad, worn out, on the verge of tears. "I don't know, but I don't think he did it. Must have been that other guy."

The uncle rose from his yard chair, his mask in his hand, and yelled at the reporters, into the night sky, "They did it, pure and simple, because they like drugs and that's it. The same reason they can't find no decent jobs. How can you work and get high? Nobody wants you.

"Now," Tony Caraman told the reporters, and his family, "lots of silly stupid people say they did that or that guys commit crimes because they are high on drugs. No way. If they get high, they like to party or just go to sleep, but they break in, hurt people and steal money because they *need* the drugs, they're *on the hunt.* They can't stand it without no drugs. I don't know how, but they can't stand the pain of not having the drugs to get them high. They are cowards," Uncle Tony shouted. "Every person has pain, different kinds.

"This is it," he said. "Listen. Ok. They need to go to their dealer to get the drugs and if they don't have no cash, and nobody gives them nothing, they have to steal. They have to pay the dealer because they are hooked on the drugs. Not one person wants to beat up an old woman. They have to do it."

Silence hung over the reporters' heads. One, at least, stirred nervously. It might go on *their* record. Not-to-ask might be the one thing that kills the dream. Kiss that job at the *Washington Post* or the *New York Times* goodbye.

Some foolish empty day, someday in the future, you never know who might, on a sleepless night, be watching a video or a "report" of this April Fool's night and hear the reporters' dark silence. Recognize their faces. Reporters are always on alert for any loophole, any way to wiggle in: They can't just sit and report. Some one of them *had to* do it, had to *ask.* It was the lone female reporter, a blonde with hair the color of beach sand on a sunny day. She stood, the spotlight dancing on her, then on Cesar's glossy white urn, back and forth as the night's wind began to pick up. She cleared her throat and asked, "Mr. *Carryman*? Thank you, you and your family for having us. We are sorry for your loss. But are you saying the need for drugs—for a 'fix'—excuses Cesar for the attack on Mrs. Gerardi? That he and the other young man *had* to attack her?"

Gloria slumped in her chair, eyes bulging. Her brother called out, even for the neighbors, for the watchers in the dark night, to hear, "Cesar was a bully but it's not because of this age, 2020. There have always been bullies. People who rather steal than be honest. Rather steal than work. My sister was a good mother. What is a mother supposed to do? She has to protect her child. She has to protect all her children. But most of the time it is the women who cover up. They want peace in the family. In the house. Sometimes, I tell you, it's a lot of jealousy with men. You wouldn't think such a thing, but I tell you *this*, the daddy will be jealous of his son, his own son. And that kid, he turns rotten. Confused, mixed up. Nothing matters except what he wants. And what he wants is somethin' to make himself feel better, you see? It could be sports, maybe college. This is the time to go one way or the other. Cesar chose the other way, the wrong way.

"After while, nothing mattered except what he needed to make himself feel good. With kids, all you can do is hope they will take only what is good and right, or maybe they won't. Maybe they will leave a family crying, or like that lady, clinging to life in the army hospital."

Tony's face was angry, yet tears ran from his eyes. He told them, "A man has got to love his family. If he don't — well, you see? Not even the mother's love can save them kids. Tell everyone we, Gloria, who lost her son, me and my wife who lost a nephew, we hope this don't happen to nobody else. *Never.*"

He wiped his face with his mask, and continued. "We pray to God, this drugs and stealing, hurting and shooting, and death, please don't let it happen to nobody else. No place. *Never again.* Thank you for coming here to be with us tonight.

"And God bless America."

Chapter eleven ~ the Requital

"Any man's death diminishes me"

For Whom the Bell Tolls

- John Donne

A week and two days after the attack on Lynsey Gerardi and the shooting deaths of Cesar Caraman and of their son, the family of Noe Alejandro gathered at their church—not for a traditional funeral service. There was no body, no casket, no unusual urn holding the ashes and bone chips of a once baptized baby, a boy so welcomed, so loved. There was no longer a boy, nothing left of a young man who, at an early age, one day left them stunned and burned, encased in an unforgivable situation, never to be the same, not in this lifetime, not at any time on this earth. It is one thing when a beloved—child, parent, sibling, baby, husband, wife—is gone, and all around you, people and priests and pastors, rabbies, teachers, uncles and aunties, speak about the sweetness, the goodness, the vivacity of the dearly departed. But how to face *this, that which must be faced, alone*? Without comfort?

For no one—from anywhere—will come. Those others, other mourners, those by blood, history, religion, from school, teams, clubs, who might otherwise be on hand this day, they will stay far away. And who can blame them? Is there not a world-wide disease all about us, in the air, on the very breath of people? Yes, it's COVID, the threat of sickness and death, that keeps cousins, pals, or workmates away. It's not merely from lack of love or compassion or propriety that they don't come. They, whoever, however, won't come today, to this place, because the truth is your baptized baby, your adorable boy, your son, was a monster.

Only by the generosity of medical research has his body earned a home. Of sorts. Some university or lab, some morgue—nearby, perhaps—will store or use his once loved body to try to discover hope or lessons that might help humanity or teach surgeons the best cuts to make. It was a decision of unease and distaste. It was a crushing blow to the Alejandro family's sense of dignity to go against tradition and faith and to send his body to the medical center—free, no fee, no cost, no recompense, no exchange, not even a name to be remembered—for research. His mother, his brother and sisters, his silent brooding father, all had agreed, he, their boy, was to have neither grace, nor a stone, not even a marking spot, a bush or a plant in some garden. His bones would not rest in the woods or in the wilds. Let him be gone, to exist only in God's eye and, in time, perhaps in his family's heart.

They sat together, but dozens or more inches apart, in the first three rows of the pews at the brand new Divine Mercy parish church in San Mateo. Fewer than ten people. In the first row, waiting, there sat the priest, Alex, who came to the United States from Argentina with a bitter taste in his mouth, and across the aisle, the brother, Peter, who had attended the boy, his brother, in the operating room, and behind and over and away from Pete were the sisters Tracy and Brittany and their tolerant husbands whose families have themselves faced tragic, nearly repugnant, funerals. The mother Anvalina sits some distance away from all the others.

Earlier this morning, Ann, wrung-out and soul-dry, considered it necessary to act, to *perform*, not in haste, not in consternation, but by design as if she were moving in a spotlight on a cold empty theater stage—she saw herself, briefly, as Elizabeth Taylor, when still alive, and thin, in *Cat on a Hot Tin Roof,* wearing a slip, pleading with her unresponsive husband Bif, or Bub. But Ann, not so thin, in her scene inside her own stark bedroom setting, wore the same similar simple lace-free white slip. If only women still wore such undergarments beneath their dresses—if only they wore dresses at all these days. All this had roved across Ann's mind, much earlier that morning, when she had indeed triumphed in her portrayal of a woman of high feeling and hysteria, threatening, demanding, possibly violent, simply and cleverly Hispanic, and sublimely magnificent. If her sullen silent husband Santiago, known as Jimmy, did not get up and get dressed and attend their son's final ceremony today at Divine Mercy Church—she told him—she didn't care what might happen to her, but she would kill him dead. Thus, Jimmy sat some distance, many unnecessary inches away from his wife at the church. But he *was* in attendance.

Again, those attending: Alex, the priest, and the priest's assistant—that is, Deacon Greg—and one uniformed deputy from the sheriff's office, deemed necessary this morning to protect the family; two sisters, two brothers-in-law, mother, and one dark brooding daddy: *Nine* persons. And Pete. *Ten.* In the very back row of church, however, one other, now making it eleven, a very blonde woman, wearing a black *mantilla* stood, knelt and and sat just as, and when, the family did. And next to the blonde, another woman sat, a distance away, Hispanic, pretty, wearing a purple pants suit, a nurse's on-duty outfit. She had wrappped herself in a baby blue knitted shawl. And behind *her*, in the narthex, the foyer, the main entrance of this very simple, sparse Catholic church—Protestant in design—a tall, pale large man hovered, standing, protectively waiting, and that makes it an even baker's dozen, thirteen in attendance. That's all there is to see, folks—except for a wall of church photographs: the pope, the bishop, the parish priest, both deacons. Group photos: the parish council, two office ladies, the parish secretary and her family, the janitors, and an expansive cork bulletin board pinned with small American flags, red, white & blue with yellow ribbons, and at least two dozen pictures of young people of the parish, smiling or stern-faced in Air Force, Army, Navy and Marine Corps dress uniforms or in varying shades of camouflage wear.

This display, stingingly painful to Ann, the mother, to see on her way into church, was painful because of her determined solidarity with those parents who could so swiftly lose children in service to their country.

"What did I do wrong," she moaned to her dusty soiled soul. "What did I do to him to hurt him, damage him so that not even one picture can be in the church, his name to be silent, why?" But no answer came to her.

Pete spoke first in the church's memorial service for Noe, and his anger was a live wire. He shaded his eyes and asked his family, the priest, the deacon, the deputy on duty, and a couple of strangers in the back, "Tell me, what can we do? We, all of us, we feel like trash. We must have come from trash. We have spawned trash, and will live with trash. We nurture trash. A man, strong, healthy, young, and he goes and attacks an old woman and tries to steal her earthly goods, listen, to me, people—that's *trash*. But why? Why did every lesson fail with him? Tell me. Because I don't know. Why must my parents suffer like this? And my sisters?" Pete

Alejandro broke down in angry tears. "My good, beautiful talented sisters, trying to build happiness, now too, are *they* trash? We all are. What woman would want to marry me? Not one. No wife, no children for me. And today—it's so strange—I am this close to saying, 'I don't care.' He did it. *We did not*. Don't come at *us*. Leave us alone. Don't come around watching us so you can figure out what went wrong. We don't care. I don't care. I wish we had the resources to leave this state, this country—although there is no better, not really." He looked up, temporally distracted and saw a friend, Rachel, Rachel Cantu, from the hospital. Probably there to try to touch base with his mother. He nodded and asked, "So, please, can you leave us alone? We are as killed, almost as dead as he is. We are sick. Please, just leave us alone."

Noe's parents—Pete's parents—declined to speak, except Ann had written some words, which the priest from Argentina read, in a heavy accent, as if it were a declaration of war on the vile racist nation where he was now forced to live, forced to drive a 2019 mid-size SUV leased for him by an unknown member of his parish, forced to live in a fashionable four-bedroom home left to the parish priest in the will of a deceased parishioner.

Father Alex began reading Ann's letter to whomever, "*I write this with tears, for my son, for Lynsey Gerardi, who has been a friend to me for many years. I hope, I pray that all goes well for her. I apologize, I beg forgiveness from God, from my family, from Noe's brother and sisters, and his dad, my husband of thirty years. Please forgive me because a mother is responsible for how her children behave, what they do in life. Leave us us alone to serve sorrow's arrows as we must. Thank you. May I say, in Christ's name, Ann Alejandro.*"

Jimmy Alejandro declined to speak at the church event, or anywhere else, and, as if she deserved more anguish, it came to be believed by many that Jimmy's silent anger would one day bring harm to his wife, his family, and to any place his silence took him. Violence, they say, begets violence. Jimmy was no longer one of them. Not the family, not the community. He was no one.

~~~

After the event at Divine Mercy, Cinnah and Preston joined Sarah at Lynsey's house for lunch in the kitchen. When Sarah heard and fully realized what had been said at the church, her heart raced. She smoothed her icy hands together, to warm them, to still them. The dizziness behind her eyes floated to her brain. She fought a wave of nausea. Clinging to her chair, she said to Preston, the number one Gerardi, and to Cinnah, the apparent number two Gerardi-to-be, and to herself, the fading number three G, "*This* is not right."

She repeated it, "*This is not right*. Cinnah, what should we do, what can we do? What are our options? Preston, what are the limits here? Think it through. That family, Ann and her husband, we know them. They didn't do anything to harm us, but this needs fixing. There are lines, limits, very thin, convoluted.

"Mother," Sarah continued—"at least from what we were able to learn last night is, she is talking, her memory is normal, whatever that means, like how would *they* know but apparently her sweet old body's just so weak. They still say she is holding her own, fighting to eat and to be alert, but what if she slips away, Preston, when we need her? I do, I need her and Jewel Norene needs her, even if—well, you know. And Jitter still needs her. This old house needs her. What are we to become without her? This is crude, but the situation is like a tube of toothpaste, there's more, there's more. I want her at my wedding, at your wedding. Why must we lose it all just because two dead guys tried to kill her?"

"So," Cinnah said, frowning, "there's still anger and helplessness in play, justified rage. How can we get past that, or can we, since our mother"—Sarah and Preston looked at her in surprise—"Miss Lynsey, that is, has suffered so much from these guys, and is *still* in danger."

Preston, with misty eyes, asked Sarah, "Can you believe how caring she is?" Sarah, of long memory, a virtual human calendar listing a lifetime of slights from her brother, wanted to slug him. Mr. Misty Eyes.

Cinnah continued. "No, I apologize. I don't feel like I should say anything. Excuse my big mouth, Sarah. I'm a newcomer, an *outlier*—is that the word?"—and Preston said, "Beats me. I don't speak French," and Sarah muttered, "You don't even speak English, not good English," and Cinnah said, "Please? Listen. I am almost ashamed of getting up and driving down here to San Mateo this morning. I had no right to go to that church. I shouldn't offer any opinions. If I had any."

Sarah said, "Well, you have two things we don't have, a job with the media and a master's degree in counseling, that's what Preston said, but he lies"—she turned toward her brother to see if her teasing was getting to him and witnessed an unusual sight: Preston was ice water melting in the sun. He had no brain, no will, when within six feet of this blonde woman. Sarah considered her own predicament: Actually to listen to Cinnah, make buddies with her or make two enemies, Preston and his gal. Do that, and I will be in a pig's trough for one very long time. Bad enough as is. Her emotions fighting her for every breath, she quietly asked

Cinnah to, "Please, dear, talk away: You are one of us." For now.

"Well," Cinnah went on, tentatively, "in a legal sense, traditional sense, we are the injured party. But that family this morning—Preston, you heard—they are bleeding. They think their entire family is trash. The young man called them trash, past and future. They feel like *trash*."

Preston was himself again. "Well, what are we going to do? I would rather no money go out. Or not much. We may have unexpected expenses getting Jewel out of Spain. I don't know. Ultimately, we might have to foot the bill for Rose and her son, maybe her husband—no tellin' how many—to get out of there. Be hospitalized somewhere. I don't want to sound callous. Just keep in mind. We have obligations. We do have limits."

"Well, sure," Sarah said. "But," she took a deep breath, "what do you say, Cinnah, maybe Preston and I, and you, should just go visit them and do something."

"I feel like a jerk," Preston said.

"No, business is business, money is money," his sister muttered. "But, not to be gaudy or too showy, but how would it be if we just go over there, now? Take some flowers. Food. If a corona illness doesn't keep them prisoners at home, and I imagine it does, then *this* makes it nearly impossible for them to go out anywhere, even to the grocery store. They need to survive this."

Cinnah was nodding, thinking.

Preston wondered aloud, "Would it be 'showy' if we sent JoJo over with food, and she could fix some meals? Y'all are the sensitive ones, not me."

Sarah said, "Let's consider that. Cinnah?"

Cinnah clapped her hands, "What a relief to get food delivered and ready-to-eat, but—"

"But *what?*" Sarah said. "Yeah, what?" Preston asked.

"Well, if you've been grieving, and if you endured that awful church thing today, you might not want a fancy stranger cooking strange food in your kitchen."

"I agree. Preston, get JoJo to cook them something *at her house*, or not, but get her moving on the shopping. Yuk, it's Saturday. But just tell JoJo how many in the family. She has smarts. She can load up. There are grandkids. But not all sweets."

"Let's do this," Preston told them. "No cooking, no cooked foods. Just a load—moderate grocery load today, and JoJo can give them a voucher for one more batch of groceries that she'll deliver, whenever."

"Or," Sarah said, "forget JoJo, I mean I love her, but she has a propensity to deliver the gossip. No, we have to do this ourselves. So, why don't you sign Ann and her family up for free year-round grocery delivery so they don't have to go in person, and we select the first delivery, then they are on their own, but with delivery pre-paid by us?"

"Sounds good," Cinnah said. "Don't want to crowd 'em."

Pres asked, "But should we still go pick up a bunch of plants, flowers, snack food, and go visit. Why, or not?"

"Not a big, big show," Sarah warned. "Let's think about Ann. She keeps a yard. Would she feel like planting what we bring? Digging in the dirt? Maybe yes, maybe no. Worse thing to have around is dying plants people sent, and all you do is sit and look at 'em because you can't even, you know, move or feel like doing anything."

Cinnah said softly to Sarah: "You've *been* there."

Sarah nodded. Then said, "By proxy. My cop thing, Cinnah," and Preston said, "I am going nuts with y'all two. Why don't I just get the nursery to do the planting?"

Cinnah laughed, "Would you want someone digging around in your yard?"

"He wouldn't care. He wouldn't even notice." Sarah smiled at Cinnah. "He's blind most of the time. Except to you. *Um.* Wait, wait, I've got it. We do like Pres' says. We pay the fee for them to get all-year-long free grocery *delivery,* Ok? We pay for today's order—which I will make—and one more delivery, paid by us, of *their* choice. They do the ordering, next time, yeah? And, y'all, we go over in person—*arrrrrg*— with flowers to tell 'em how wonderful we are. Noooo."

Cinnah: "How about this—one of you calls the mom. No surprise visits. Let her say when—"

Sarah interrupted. "Sorry, sorry. But we do need to know *when.* I mean, should we go today? Can we pull that off, like right now? Don't forget, tomorrow, Sunday morning, we're going to go to San Antonio when they move Mother from SAMMC to the rehab—but they changed that. Still we need to be there, in the afternoon. Only chance to see her, when they move her."

Preston agreed. "Right. Tomorrow. They may change it again, if something happens. But if they want to move her. They want her to be ready, as we do. Cinnah, come with us. We can't get inside but we thought we'd see her when they bring her out of one hospital—"

Sarah interrupted, "*Oh, holy cow!* Brother, you are brilliant. We'll beat the system. After they load her in the ambulance, we'll drive real fast to get to the rehab place before the ambulance gets there, and see her twice!"

"Group *hug*," Cinnah said, "no, wait. Group *chest pound!* No, Preston. Get away, you idiot. And I was just about to say sweet things about you. But listen, listen. Call the mom. For what time? Make it tomorrow, Sunday, at five, Ok? I need to go home right now, you guys. Preston, stop. Why does he always cry about everything?"

Sarah nodded, said, "It's how he gets his way" Cinnah told him, "Cry all you want, I don't care, see? But make sure the son of the family, Pete, the OR nurse, will be there, all of the family. Both of you. Take some pretty blooming something, flowering plants. Talk to them, talk some more. Try to, you know, make nice, the two of you. Expect rejection. When all seems cool, tell the mom about the food thing. Preston will have it all set up. But y'all, I need to *get.* I am 'zero at the bone' about this morning. My heart hurts. Thanks, Sarah. Preston, I'll see you next week, on Monday, if you are lucky. Y'all, I just need to go home to my son and play with the dog."

"*Dog?*" Preston hooted. "You never told me you have a *dog.* Ok, we're done here. No cute announcements. I can't go steady with a dog…"

Sarah made a fist. Cinnah yelled, "*Dog?* Dog, is it? *You* may go steady with any old *dog*, sir, but not with me!"

"Y'all are goin' steady? Do people do that?"

"Some," Cinnah said. "Ones who haven't grown up yet."

Preston grabbed Cinnah, and studied her left hand. "Is this your way of tellin' us you want something on this finger, a plain gold band, perhaps."

"Plain gold band?" Cinnah questioned him, "*Plain?* On me? *My hand?*" She, a little bit, not much, and sister Sarah called him names: Tightwad, cheapskate.

He continued, "If you two banchees will stop that, I will tell you. I saw a plain gold band in my cigar box—"

"*Cigar? Cigar box?*" Cinnah picked up her bag, ready to haul out of there. "You smoke cigars? My dog and I are both allergic to cigars. It's over. I'm gone."

Sarah told them, "I hope y'all don't charge admission. I want a refund. *Eeeeek,*" she complained. "Don't start kissin' on her. COVID! Go buy a ring. I-I need to lie down. Good grief! And bye-bye, all. Love ya, Cinnah. Next time. Preston, grow up, dude."

After Cinnah left, sister and brother still just sat at the table. The brains, the spirit of the three, had departed the building. Preston said, "I have a little problem."

Sarah looked at him hard. "*What* problem? Are you going to admit to five illegitimate little bas—"

"Mother's dog," Preston told her. "Little Dog," he said. "Stupid dog that was here that day. Owners don't answer calls. Dog's been in the vet's all this time. We're paying for a dog's vacation. Sarah, you listening?"

"Nice dog," she mused. "Needs a home. What if we just *happen* to have Little Dog with us when we visit Ann?"

"What? Then abandon him. Just leave him there?"

"You got a better idea? Cinnah has a dog. We don't need a dog. Mother can't stand dogs. He'd starve to death with us. And who doesn't just love-love-love a little doggie-dog?"

Chapter twelve ~ the Ribbon Party

"...like an untimely frost..."

Romeo and Juliet

-William Shakespeare

One month after her attack, two days after her release from the rehab hospital, Lynsey was parked in a cushioned high-back chair on her porch, overlooking the backyard and the gate to the cemetery. Sarah had selected a long black and white dress for her mother and they had topped it off with a bright red silk shirt. "Old lady duds," Lynsey said, but what the heck. She waved her mask in the air. "How do y'all like my mask?" It was a matching bright red.

On her lap she held her laptop covered in roses and lilacs.

"Should have worn not *red*," she groused. "Maybe pink. But I don't have a picky bask. *Mask*," she said. "Shee whiz. Ever *thang* change." Since the attack, after her surgeries and procedures, at home again, she had tried the first day to compose some little diddly-wop on her laptop. Not only was it massively difficult, no dice. Her readers had vanished, done a runner. She wrote to them again yesterday, come back. Come back, y'all. Maybe they would—just this morning, she had noticed things. Like fingerprints, and what could be fine crumbs. What's up with that? Had her readers begun to return? Been looking for her? Praise Jesus. But be careful, don't get tricked, she told herself. Don't give in to wishful thinking. But whoever y'all are, some invisible persons, or force, don't be evil. Be a Godly force. Anyhow, someone, somebody a little messy had started getting into her laptop. Great happiness and thanksgiving for even one reader. Word of mouth, they'll return. A laptop using the cloud, the sky, makes it easy. New readers will come.

Mail had piled up while she was in the hospital that she did not see until her last week at the rehab place. A couple of cards were from Red Clay, and one long letter. He'd told her a great deal about his life, and while the best she could do now was scratch him a few text messages, he answered so quickly, and now, he was coming again to San Mateo. On Wednesday, the coming week, the 29th of April. She would see him soon, and this time she wanted him to stay at the house, sleep in her room, with her. He had said whatever she wanted but to remember he'd have "the kid' with him. It took forever; those text messages jump all around so much, but she'd told him—tried to tell him—she had a room for "the kid" on the other side of the house and if Red Clay didn't like that, then "the kid" could sleep in Lynsey's big soft comfy room and she and Mr. Clay would sleep on the other side of the house in the store room. She was being brassy, flirtatious, but it was a hoot. They were fitting again, after almost 70 years.

And now, a neighborhood meeting. Please, no. She began again. Thinking. Was it 70 years, or sixty? If thinking was hard, simple arithmetic was pure dee murder. It had been 1952, not 1962. She counted on her fingers, by tens. Almost 70 years. If math had become hard, spelling was hell itself. She tried. She wanted to get into the swing of the laptop again. The thing could spell, it could tell her when something was wrong, it jumped and shook its head if she typed her password wrong. What good are passwords? Big Brother. Watchers. Communists. *Hooligans.* She laughed to herself over what she had told Sarah about her missing readers: "It's like going to confession and the priest says, 'Keep talking, I'm just going out for a snack.'" With Sarah, no response. The girl always thought her mother was up to something. "I swear," Lynsey muttered. But now, new life. A wounded, demented loving new life. She was determined to fight on, even to write her own obituary. Maybe this evening. Or in the morning. "You must read *this*, you snoops. It's me own obit." With a big headline. In the paper. In the *San Mateo Argus.* Wow.

She was thinking: I'm happy now, I can retire. Let Sarah and old Pres' run the show. I want to sit and ponder the difference between *sample* and *example.* Even if you have all your marbles, English is a maze. A spider web. A flowing river. Logical, unless you want to get picky. No, it's not a pretty-sounding lingo, but it is soft, not harsh, and just consider its use worldwide, in science, in medicine, in film, well, let's not brag on that. Ah. Suddenly, her mind opened to a joke about an obit. Remember, remember? Nope, but she knew writing her own obituary was the last thing she wanted to do.

Plus, she was dying to tell someone, anyone, about the mani and pedi she got at rehab. Lynsey had thanked the precious nurse who stayed late to polish and paint her fingernails and toenails a lovely pink. "Hey," she told that nurse, "You know how the pedi was Ok but the *mani* was too little, get it?"

Suddenly Jefferson Bergeron stood arms-length from her, right there on her San Mateo veranda, asking, *"Lyns' Ann, why you actin' so stupid? No more stories. Your mother never never joke around all nasty about men things."*

Right. Daddy was right. She could at least keep her mouth shut. Be silent. No more jokes. Or memories.

"Daddy, wait," she called to him in the afternoon air, "I want to explain about Red Clay. Don't be hurt that I never told you. Daddy, I have agreed never to go to the hospital again. No more doc appointments, just tele-talks. It's like Redux. Like we used to. *Rabbit Redux.* Daddy, remember John Updike, you liked him. He's dead. Still dead. Forever silent. Don't go. Don't go, Daddy, I need to tell you, now I see what a cruel business I have led, and called it Jitterbug. I got rich off of those sorrowful circles. Life and death. It shames me now. Now I am *there*, Daddy. *Me.* I'm in Jitterbug, in hospice. Waiting for the grim reaper, for my faith to unveil the face of—oh, *quelle surprise*—"

"Preston, honey," Lynsey cooed, clutching a moment of reality. "Now, honey, tell me"—she clutched his hand, decided not to kiss it—"are we havin' some kind of a neighborhood meetin' or else, did Sarah just park me here to draw flies?" And he told her, "No, Mother, not a meeting. It's a party. For just a few people."

He motioned toward a blonde lady, young in a flowery dress, reached for her hand, gently pulled her to him for a romantic pose. Lynsey saw how tall her son was, still manly at 62, 63, in a black mask. The lady's flowery mask—matched the fabric of her dress. Flowery. Lynsey stared. Yep. The mask's fabric was the same as the girl's dress. "She *sews*," Lynsey announced and Pres' said, "Mother, this pretty thing is, *ah,* Cinnah—"

"*Why? Say what?*" Lynsey chewed the inside of her mask.

"Mother," Preston began again, "it's a, well, a secret, but this is my friend. Mother, this—is my dear *Cinnah*."

"Oh, honey," Lynsey whispered as fiercely as possible to the blonde girl in the flowers, "I apologize. *Him?* Never mind what he calls you. That boy is a poor judge of anyone's soul because he has had a noddin' and a fiddlin' relationship with sin as long as we've had him."

Sarah stepped up. "*Mother,*" she said, but Lynsey, still stuck on sin, told everyone, "Puts me in mind of the Salem witch hunts and the Scarlet '*B*,' doesn't it you, Missus *Cinnah*?"

Sarah said, "Mother, don't you mean the Scarlet '*A*'?"

"Sin always gets an 'A,' so sad, *wink, wink.*"

"I was about to say, *Mother,* we can only have about ten people at a time today. And we're all wearing masks."

Lynsey waited, silently. Mask or not, it was nice to be outside. A lukewarm day. Yesterday, they said, the high had been ninety degrees. Texas weather. And she remembered: No jokes. No wise cracks. Humbled, she said aloud, "Ten people. That's a nice size." And then it tumbled out, "I was wondering if the empty chairs were a hint. Like the horse with no rider, or do I mean the riderless horse? Anybody know? A horse with no rider? Just a pair of shiny backassward *boots?*"

"No," Sarah corrected her. "People *are* coming. The chairs are set a little far apart right now because of the virus. We're having a little party, but first, C-cinnah is going to record this." Lynsey was shaking her head no, no way, let's stop calling the girl *Cinnah*. My children are so damn rude. With a finger over her mask-covered lips, she meant shhh, Sinner, don't admit to a thing. And then Sarah announced, "FaceTime with Jewel."

"Really? Time with Jewel?" Lynsey's voice was somber. "Thank you, thank you. So, who is coming?" she asked, just as Preston stepped out onto the veranda, holding Sarah's open laptop. He placed it on his mother's lap, on top of Lynsey's laptop, the second-hand one, and clamped earphones over her head, careful of her hair.

"So you can hear," he said, and she agreed, "Sure."

With the set-up complete, Preston told her, "Ok, go ahead." Lynsey pulled down her mask, and enunciated carefully, calling out, "Jewel Norene, hello, precious, hello, hello. I am home from the hospital, two of them, and sitting on the back porch." She stopped, and turning, smiled sweetly at Cinnah. She listened to her American-born daughter who had lived in Scotland for 37 years, but now was hiding out from her lump of a husband at the home of *her* only child, Rose, Rosa. In Spain, the great horror pit-dog-pit virus-ridden COVID unsanitary stankhole of the earth. "But tell us," Lynsey pleaded, "how is it in beautiful *España* where everyone just *loves* to hug and kiss so much, unlike us putrid, uh, I mean, *puritanical* old Americans?"

She listened and asked, "So, you all spend a lot of time in the garden. The sun—yes, how is Mistress Rosa, my granddaughter? Oh, she's in the house?

"Works at home? Sounds good. Sure. You bet. Busy, busy. Next time, oh, for certain. Next time we'll talk. Ah, I wish you all great happiness on this day of *San Jorge*. It was yesterday? On April 23, 24? Ooo, no celebrations this year. No, I just happened to remember. I remember many useless things, not that St. George is useless. Tell us about my great grandson, little Juan Carlos." She listened. "So, they let them out for soccer? He loves soccer? And animals." To everyone standing around, twiddling their thumbs but listening with both ears, she whispered, "They have two dogs." She listened again. "And a kitten." She held up three fingers.

"Well, we have social distancing, yes. And now, the masks. Yes, they say, 'Stay home. Save a life.' Absolutely, pray for a vaccine. A cure." She was silent, listening. "I am! I am well. Yes, a month ago. Not much. Sure, I can walk, but I don't know about the journal. Not so much anymore. Sarah is starting a journal, I'm stopping. Do you keep one? *Oohh*, I am so glad, Jewel, but keep it private, you don't want—"

Lynsey frowned, listening. "Now, here's what I hope you will do—" A long silence. "Sure. You can talk to Sarah. In a minute, Ok? Don't want to give you up yet. I like your hair, short and sassy. Nice color. Yes, Sarah's right here. And our *Sinner*, but who am I to judge, you know who said that? Yes, Preston is getting married. Right, and her little eight-year-old boy, they will be moving in. Yes. Same age as Juan Carlos. Maybe they can play those video games together. Over the great pond." She listened again. "No, no. Don't cry. Not true. We'll always have room for you, always room for my Jewel. If you come, we'll build on, add a gym, a dance studio. An apartment." She listened. "There'll always be room…

"Wait. Wait," she pleaded. "I tell you. As soon as President *Bush* lifts the travel restrictions, it'll be pretty soon, and I'll have Preston get you a flight to Austin. Sure. Ok. You can talk to her." She listened again and then, her face showing stress, dismay, as if shocked or pinched, she said, "Oh! He is? But—? Oh, he's driving. *Poof*. I clean forgot you can drive—can you?—from the UK to Spain? Yes, I see, I understand, my girl." Lynsey's pain was disturbingly visible. She was flailing with the agony of reality, floundering, drowning, in front of all, on camera. *Glub, glub, glub. Down with me.*

She opened her mouth, trembling, scaring Sarah and Preston's blonde woman. Yet Lynsey, for all her deshablement, was silently, softly, repeating, "Father Jesus," over and over. Her heart, her psyche, sought *Lupita*, the *Virgen de Guadalupe*, who also once lost her child. Like Jewel, he wasn't in the wagon. And in union with Anthony, patron saint of lost items, lost people, she whispered, *"Help me, I am lost,* I once was lost." And, for over eighty years, since her school days in Saverne, when Mother was sick, she had, when in trouble, turned to Padre Pio. Once a simple Italian priest, he bore the *stigmata:* That is, he bled from his hands, his feet, his side, bled like Christ's own wounds. She said, *"Padre Pio, help me.* Help me, help us. People don't know. Don't believe, don't care."

Lynsey's face burned, her eyes were hard and unmoving, lips dry, trembling, her cheeks aflame. She turned her face toward Cinnah. Their eyes met. She said, "Help me." Cinnah stopped filming. This thing with Jewel had to end. "Don't hang up," Lynsey said in a rough whisper, *"Daddy* wants to talk."

She handed Sarah's open laptop away as if it were boiling. Cinnah gently removed Lynsey's earphones and Preston took it all indoors. Sarah stood, torn between following her brother and hearing whatever Jewel wanted to tell her or staying with her mother. Ashamed of her pause, she fluffed up Lynsey's snow white curls, found her mask, and helped her mother as she lay her head back on her chair's padding, then to one side. With heavy hands, Lyns' worked to adjust her mask. Eyes closed, she was surprised to still see the sun, the red-blood, white-bright sun. Jewel was going back to her horrible and abusive husband. Lynsey fought with herself; acceptance of this old new pain negates hope, doesn't it? "Dear God, I wanted to see her one last time. It's not to be. She wants him, an abuser. There is no choice for Jewel, COVID and dependency keep her away, but I thank you, dear God, you held me up. I saw her. She is in your hands. She is mine no longer." She kept her eyes closed.

Lynsey struggled. Busy with a stack of papers, she had to stop, car horns honking, and race outside to chase after that wild little child running into the street. That girl needed a spank. Spanks were Ok for kids running across streets, but Lynsey knew she couldn't do it. Truth was, she'd be willing to knock Sarah Maddy's block off, any day of the week, although she never had. But Jewel, no. I was weak, indulgent. Now she is weak, wrapped around a man who will destroy her, nip by nip by nip.

Lynsey pictured her daughter as she had been on the laptop, old, tired, desperate, short-haired, too blonde, *cheap,* and she felt hopeful: The girl could still learn.

Yep, misery is the best teacher. Let her learn that love without reason is abuse, and of course reason without love creates a monster. She opened her eyes and decided, "I, for example, will *think* this through." She sat up, no more napping. "I will love my way through this, this mite of trouble." She wondered, which is stronger? Reason or love? Reason. Reason is the *winnah.* She turned to see Preston's wife-to-be, watching her again, behind her flowered mask. Cinnah, the *winnah.* Their eyes met and smiled over their masks.

"Daddy, you would like her." No one heard Lynsey say this, and she marveled at Preston's friend, with a name that sounds like sin and hair that looks like the palest of sunlight. And how could her eyes, the green shade of a flowing Texas river, understand Lynsey's thoughts without words. Mother of Jesus, help me control myself today. Help us, help Preston, to keep Cinnah and her young son, Kevin. May life in this house be blessed.

In the military hospital, she had enjoyed video visits with the Vietnamese-born American priest, Captain Dung. Before she left for rehab, he visited her in person. He heard her confession—it wasn't easy—and he placed the Eucharist, the bread, into her hand, a tiny piece so she didn't choke. He told her don't worry about what she says. Easy for him to say. He didn't seem to catch much of what she told him. But after his visit, she felt high, in a rush to die. Yet she lived. Even so, she liked Dung.

When Lynsey focused her eyes again, JoJo was in the kitchen. Big as life. Brighter. Yoli, Magda, both Guzman by name, US citizens, or on the way, and Margaret Conant were buzzing about in masks and gloves. Margaret and her husband had made a dozen wood and plastic gold-and-green sunflowers with funny eyes and wearing masks. On her way in, they had planted the sunflowers at social distances around Lynsey's front yard. Cinnah brought Lynsey photos of the sunflowers on her cell.

"I *love* the sunflowers, Garet," Lynsey, mask aside, murmured to her, "I have never been able to get 'em to grow. In Saverne, where I come from, man once had sunflower fields—commercial, it was business—and those sunflowers, way taller than me, would turn their faces to the sun. All day, turnin' faces, in unison. They say that's the way we should be, following God's truth. Don't know what happens in the dark, maybe they face each other and start fussing."

"Or kissing," Garet suggested through her mask.

Surprised that someone was listening, Lynsey told her potential protéegée, "Well, I love y'all's sunflowers and I know they'll behave." Garet gave a thumb's up and sat on the porch rather near Mrs. Gerardi who was, clearly, out of breath. But never happier. Almost never. Fausto and Shirley arrived quietly and took up three chairs. Cora Emerson was with them and she had brought a dozen yellow roses, enough for everybody to have one, or almost. Lynsey heard someone say, "...*they canceled Fiesta, in San Antonio* ..." Someone else said, "...*canceled the state fair in Dallas*..." "...*should have called off Mardi Gras*..." "What about *graduations*..." "...sad how *funerals* are postponed..."

After a lull, Lynsey waved her red mask and first chose to greet the sheriff's wife. "My precious Shirley. We are together at last! You look so pretty, trim and graceful. Staying home, fixing, that's what the sheriff said. I love to do that too. Self-directed work. Never gets boring, just fixing and a-doing. Thanks for coming."

"Cora, my Cora." Lynsey sighed, when she saw CE, at a distance, it seemed. In a strained voice, she said, "Cora. My dear brave friend. My savior. You and Jesus. Oh, what I wouldn't give to hug you. Or come on, you're slim enough, come over and sit on my lap. Except everybody says stay a mile away from me. And my cooties."

"Well, Mother, we have a way," Sarah said, "but first, put that mask on, and keep it on." Taking a spool of lavender ribbon from her basket of *things,* she gave one end of the ribbon to her mother and the other end to Cora. Then with the yellow roses being passed around, she changed her mind and—stopping to adjust her mother's red mask over her ears—took back the lavender ribbon, gave it to Cinnah and Lynsey, and presented the yellow ribbon end to Cora, and Lynsey. Some applauded, and cheered. Sarah said it was the hardest job she'd had in years. It was almost true.

"'Just give a little tug,'" Sarah said, explaining how the ribbon deal works, "'when you want a little hug.' I know. Kind of ticky-tacky, I know. But it might be pretty, like a

May pole. Preston actually suggested the 'hug tug' thing."
He called out from inside, "Preston did *not*."

"That hug apply to me?" Faus asked and Sarah assured him it
did. She connected the Dellheims and Lynsey together with
a long leash of doubled white ribbon, Lynsey holding onto
the middle of the length. Almost everyone played the game
of trying to ignore what everyone else was noticing: The
sheriff's eyes were flooded with tears. How long could one
man cry? He had been crying for a month. Sarah floated away
and placed a box of tissues on his chair arm and a dry mask,
a paper one. Then, she connected Garet and Lynsey together
with a golden ribbon, reminding each of Garet's sunflowers.
"What if I drop my end? Of the ribbon?" Lynsey asked and
Sarah snapped at her, "We'll pick it up." *Wo*, sorry.

Preston returned, took his seat, and Sarah gave her mother
and brother opposite ends of bright blue ribbon.

Sarah gave her mother a pink ribbon and seated herself holding
the other end. Lyns' said, "I have blue. gold, and lavender,
and pink, and white. And yellow. What else?"

Yoli and Magda and Lynsey got a doubled red ribbon. Again,
Lyns' Ann got to hold the folded middle of the length. And
JoJo, and Lynsey, got bright green.

A surprise, Gina, the new mother, stood just inside one of
the tall glass windows of Melody House, holding her daughter,
named Lynsey Ann. With Gina, standing, rocking the baby,
those outside on the veranda simply watched, remembering
other infants, other new moms. Lynsey thought is was like
Mary, the Madonna, holding baby Jesus. Everyone sat still,
watching, chatting into the distance, comfortably holding
their ribbon leading to Lynsey's fistful of color. *Gina*. Little
Gina Bosewell. Lynsey was remembering how it started,

right here, on this porch. That girl that Hollis loved, Melissa, would bring Gina over with her to visit and the little girl would swirl and run and jump to music only she heard. What a wonderful child, now a mother. It used to be so many came here, to Melody Street. No more. But she shook it off. Red Clay is coming this week. At last Lynsey spoke again, "Fausto, sir, do you remember the first time you came to this house? As an adult?"

"Yes, I do," he said. "It was a Sunday. In August."

"Indeed, it was, my most honorable friend. Now. No crying. It's a party. JoJo, sweetie." Lynsey tried to clap her hands. "Do we have anything for these folks to eat?"

JoJo, already a bright blossom, re-bloomed at the opportunity to talk food. "We have individually wrapped spice cake just wallowing in, er, *cinna*-mon, nutmeg, ginger, allspice, cloves and what-all, with a to-die-for white icing. And thanks to Yoli, we have Mexican sugar cookies, so pretty, also in baggies. And we have baggies of fresh-sliced fruit, and nuts. Good for you, good for your tummy. Please, on your way, take some, and don't forget the kids back at the house. Oh, you bet, sure, the sheriff says he is 'a kid back at the house.'" JoJo continued, "Help yourselves to a Root Beer, on the table. And fun, fun, look, we have Cracker Jacks! In the box, in honor of our Cracker Jack lady, Miz Lynsey. You know. People at my house said it'd be better if I sprinkled the cracker jacks on top of the icing."

But Fausto had begun a happy hum, waving his arms like a band director, singing, *"I'll tell you what you can do: Take me out to the ball game—take me out with the crowd,"* and high-pitched voices joined him; JoJo, hands on substantial hips, tried a tap dance step, and then they got loud: *"Buy me some peanuts and Crack-er Jacks, I don't care if we nev-er get back, so let's root, root-root for Lynsey, Preston and Cinnah and everybody.."*

"JoJo," Sarah was sending her voice across the veranda, "those Cracker Jacks? You ever hear how people told Michelangelo he should have painted the Sistine Chapel black and white?"

"And put clothes on them all," Garet added.

Lynsey laughed sweetly, and held back on one or two smartass comments she was tempted to make. Instead she told Garet, "That's so funny," and Garet nodded her head in happiness and in glowing self-esteem.

"JoJo," Lynsey hollered hoarsely at her chef, "Sarah is right." She said that because indirectly she wanted to draw Sarah out. She was sort of new, a bit shy. She hoped San Mateo would make her daughter feel welcome. God knows, all those horrible years in Houston was enough to kill off anybody's humanity.

Lynsey had been waiting fifty to sixty years to see Preston or Sarah, either one, to show the *pizza pizzazz* of their father. Neither had married. Should both have grandchildren. With shock, she decided—what, *hey*—Preston and Sarah are quite fine, as they are. Often reticent, contained, kind of sparkling, fun, you know, on the back burner, even if they do tend to say stripped-down rude bare-knuckled insensitive things. "Dear God, the poor foolish *tings* are exactly like me."

The truth was her elderly children were subtly powerful, kind, and sincere, but they had that inherited trait: If there was a rotten stinking thing to say or a dirty thought unexpressed, they were on it like lightning after thunder. As their mother, she appreciated their recent restraint.

"What are those things," she asked herself. Good fruits or gifts? They make a person unbelievably attractive because, whatever, but these *gifts* are free to every damn person alive who wants them, not to commit murder or to run drugs or whores. No, no, but these gifts are infinitely more powerful than our inherited genes or that other thing, a new thing, they like to talk about, DNA, which helps cops identify dead bodies and unknown folks. *Why have I never discussed this with Sarah?* I will do it tomorrow, first thing.

Anyhow, with these gifts—get this—you can forget the burning stinking guilt implicit in the question, Do we blame nature or nurture? *Goody pie.* She was polka-dot tired and was seeing silver spots everywhere she looked.

"You understand," Lynsey drew in a breath, and thought she might be telling someone, her readers, or Yoli, or Fausto, maybe even Red Clay, "that even with this stuff, DNA, the great huff, the dither would no longer be about crazy parents.

"Here's the deal. It would be about accepting these gifts."

She had a moment of clarity—like from the cloud—and recited the names of the gifts: Love, joy, peace, patience, kindness, goodness, joy, forbearance, gentleness, modesty, and self-control. And *warsh* your hands, but wait. Lynsey felt pleasure and immediately asked herself, "What's wrong?"

"Oh, looky here," Lynsey purred behind her mask—her eyes dry, immobile, refusing to move. Assuming the role of a fat half-blind momma cat, she wished she had the guts, the *gift*, to show her children, her literal & legal offspring, how much she liked them—or what? Do I hear something? In my head was, oh, could it be sum *bith* me: Why can't I *givethle* them affection that comes to me for others?

Ok, buzz and purr, purr and buzz. "Oh, I see Yoli. Look, we are red-ribboned together, the color of life. And Magda! How pretty. How's Aiden? Loves your phone? Tries to text? What a cutie. Gonna be president some day, just watch."

Magda stood, her mask hanging prettily from one ear. Motioning her Squad Two partner, she said, "Miss Lynsey, me and Garet have a surprise." She stopped and, lightly stomping one foot, mouthed, "Garet. Come-here-to-me."

Garet was untwisting her golden ribbon, coming closer to Magda who began again. "Garet and I are going to sing a special for you. We have been practicing on our cells. You will hear the real music from Garet's Ipad, pod. This is a very old song, a hundred years. Wait. Garet wants to speak."

In a San Mateo nonosecond, Garet's mask vanished. She beamed into the missing spotlights, the absent Music Town Tonight cameras and announced, "Look at me, I'm shaking," but she went on smiling, wide-eyed. "Miss Lynsey, you're from Texas. Magda's from Mexico and I'm from Lafayette, Louisiana. And we're goin' to sing one of my favorites, *Allons à Lafayette*. It's Cajun."

Magda said, it seemed, between her teeth, "The iPad is now ready," but Garet, smiling brightly, again announced as if to a microphone, "Let's say hi to Mr. Lee Benoit and his band." Everyone was looking at her. She lifted her eyebrows and said, "He's from Rayne, not Lafayette, and I know him. Well, I don't *know* him but I have seen him in person. He's won a lot of awards. People say he's better than Lynyrd Skynyrd and Hank Williams combined, somethin' like that. Yeah, so the song we're doing is pretty old, but you should hear my very *fav*, 'Constant Sorrow' or 'The Visit,' wow, Ok, I'll hurry. But his music will make everybody feel better in COVID. It's *merveilleux, formidable, c'est vrai, mes amies, oh-kay!*" They were ready. Magda said, "From the beginning" and Lynsey said to herself, "Rooted in Acadiana," and some guests danced together, and others danced alone *together*. Yoli sat, grinning. Lynsey's hands were dancing in front of her, never dropping a ribbon. Inside a tall window, Gina was rocking the younger Lynsey. "This is your first dance, *maro balaka*"—she whispered in memory of so many Indian babies—"never forget this music. Or this day, little one." It went like this:

https://youtu.be/m6mfsb6eggM. (*YouTube:* Lee Benoit, "Allons a Lafayette"

Allons à Lafayette, c'est pour changer ton mon.

Let's go to Lafayette to change your name

On va t'appeler Madame, Madame Canaille Comeaux.

We will call you Mrs. Mischievous Comeaux.

Petite, t'es trop mignonne pour faire ta criminelle.

Honey, you're too pretty to act like a tramp.

Lynsey, smiling and laughing, wished Red Clay had been here, and when the clapping stopped, and the girls looked to Lynsey, she, hand over her heart, told them, "The most fun, thank you. The best!"

Out of the corner of her eye, she recognized Garet's husband standing in the old rose garden next door—he didn't appear to be too recently covered in bruises from a beat-down by his wife; he had only been trying to listen and take video. Amazing, the human heart. Amazing, that Sarah and her surveillance team had not hogtied him and hauled him off to the hoosegow.

Lynsey tugged Preston's ribbon and together they motioned Herb Conant to come on in, join the group. Preston loped to meet him, to unlock the side gate. Lynsey blew him a kiss and with both hands blew kisses to Garet and Magda who were being silly, laughing, posing for pictures.

The ribbons, under Sarah's watchful eye, were jiggling and flowing, and Lynsey saw Faust and how he was smiling even though his face was sobbing wet, his tears shining in the late afternoon sunlight. She felt her own face. It was hot, but her hands and stupid feet—were like ice. She looked at her hands. Not shaking, but heavy.

Silly things were lead weights. The skin between the ribbons looked as if it had been painted or dipped into a clear shade of lilac. Lavender skin.

At times the sun, through the oak trees, speckled itself on her and Sylvia Ann, then trailed away. Time was on its unchanging path with sundown overcoming them. In the shade, there, a pretty girl was lyin' back, wearin' a satin dress. *Mother. Mother.* Mother wore satin. But why do they say there's *a room, where you do what you don't confess?* Why, why say such terrible words? Lynsey felt a crushing sorrow in the pit of her person. It was that time, the golden hour. Coming. Going. The tiny lights, in bushes, twisted around tree trunks, mingled savagely with the arriving dusk. Would Red Clay like her house? Need to do some planting, hibiscus, but damn 'biscus never bloom, begonias better, Ok, and herbs for JoJo. God and man, God and his terrible gifts. Preston gave her a nod. Now? Ok, sure. Lubbock could wait. She'd think about all that later. In a strained voice, but with a resolve built on a pre-arranged planning session with him, and Sarah Maddy—but she could not remember why—Lyns' spoke into space, to Squad Two. She was a pleased animal, so full of steady happiness, a wild fox or a spoiled house cat *murring* to her babies.

"Magda, sweetie, go talk to my son next week. See about taking classes this summer on, what is it, pres?'

"Online from the community college." Lynsey was nodding in agreement. She butted in, "Magda. He will fix it up. You don't pay one dime. He will get you all you need. No problems. School, yes?"

Magda's eyes were large, her face pale. Then she flashed a questioning, almost flirtatious, smile at the old man whose gut she had, about a month ago, considered slicing into with her switchblade knife. Yoli was grinning. And anyone attentive to what's happening now was enjoying this.

The Guzman ladies couldn't stop hugging each other. School was the best thing. Lynsey wanted to remind everyone: They say an education, some learning, any learning, is something nobody can steal or take away from you, but she was sinking. And it was an obscure thought, about formal education anyhow. Debatable.

Lynsey managed to say, with a tug on Magda's ribbon, "Any classes you want. Aiden can be with you at home. Study music, or nursing, or numbers, ohhh, promise me, Magda? And, I think we can find a laptop for you." She tapped her own and winked at the girl, so young, already the mother of a little boy. Then—she spoke. "Margaret, Garet. I love the name, and the young person you are. We know you are smart as a whip. If you want, Garet, go see Preston at the Jitterbug office over near the university. You all know where. Magda? Garet, right? Maybe on Monday. Or Tuesday. Garet, he wants to offer you a job. A different Jitter-job," she said, enjoying this, "we'd like you, maybe so, in the office, managing schedules. Or, with clients, you going to visit the elderly. Your choice, Garet. See what that good-looking husband of yours says, go see what Preston says—I might go with you, one way or another—and, well, Ok." Glancing at her son, she declared, "Preston is also kind of good-looking"—those who could hear laughed. "And then you, Garet, you say what you want to do because you are a Louisiana girl, right?" Garet nodded, and bobbed around like a masked cheerleader. A crying masked happy cheerleader.

"One more change in the company. Preston says," and Lynsey stopped: Who made him boss? Oh, I did: Me. "Listen, Preston says, with COVID and what not. It's time we make improvements. In the look of some of our offices. That's six locations. That might change. Yoli, *Yolanda Maria Guzman.* We hope you will accept this job. There will be money for you to spend." Lynsey felt chest pain, or gas. Yoli was listening intently, *how, where?*

Lynsey said, "Now this is actually two jobs, Yoli. You will need to travel to our offices, spend the night, perhaps your husband or one of the children can go with you, but also you will be the Manager of all the Squads, keeping track, hiring new Squad members, teaching them, like that. We love you, Yoli. Don't retire. We want to keep you, to pay you more. Of course, talk with Sergio, and the family. It will be different for you and Magda, not being together all day." Yoli, who said not a word, was gently pulling on the red ribbon that connected her to Lynsey, and Lyns' Ann, swallowing tears, understood. She, herself, needed a minute's rest. "Y'all talk. Let's hear from you folks."

Cora, in her school teacher voice, piped up, saying nice things about Lynsey who, honestly, could not hear, but she knew that CE was thanking the Sheriff and was saying how happy she and her daughter Luz were to get to know Deputy

Joey Galvan. "They get along so well," Cora said. Lynsey heard that. "Code talk," she said to herself: "The love bug. Merciful God, *I've got the love bug, help me.*" Cora was saying Joey's uncle—and Lynsey thought, "Uncle? Oh! Uncle Bern. Aunty Pop, can y'all come over and play Spoons with us tonight, see the ribbons, set off some fireworks?"

But some lady was saying that *Joey's* uncle had "been there," had been wounded in Fallujah, back in 2004—Cora's voice never changed. And, she was saying, some other veterans from our wars had accepted her into their *bus* group. PTSD group. Did anybody remember Kelly Petrus, Cora asked, a medic who had been wounded? In 2010. His family's from here. A shrug traveled the group, but Lynsey knew Ed and Rosemary Petrus, and their little grandson is Kelly.

"He's quite the artist, cartoonist," the lady was saying. "Turns out Kelly is in discussions with *Stars & Stripes*. So, fingers crossed, everybody."

Lynsey crossed her fingers, not losing a single ribbon.

"He has some," Cora paused to pat her face, "some hard-hitting comic strips about military life, like some guys are in the hospital, and here comes big old COVID."

Lynsey said, "Soldiers first." And Cora was saying, "My life has has gone from that day, sandpaper to velvet." And Lynsey also said, "Sandpaper to velvet."

Fausto's turn. He stood. "You are hearing this from me, and Shirl first. *This is my last term as sheriff*. It's been almost fifty years. And much as I love it, this virus has made me and Shirley see life from a different view. I will not stand for re-election this year. Oh-*ho*," he teased.

"Y'all want to know who my replacement is. I see it in your eyes: 'Sit down, you old coot, who've we got in your place?' Well, it might be time for a lady sheriff, some lady right here, right now."

Lynsey put her hand up, said, "I'll do it."

And they laughed. Oh! *The nerve of some people,* but quick- as-a-running-deer and realizing what Faus was up to, Lynsey put her hand up again and said, "Sarah Maddy can do it." She wanted to say she's a lady cop! She wanted to have enough vocal power to ask, "Hey, y'all. Do you ever see Sarah's double, her character, in that TV series, *CI Brainworks*? They say that Alexis Somebody, the star, looks exactly like Sarah, a young Sarah, of course, and don't you love the way her team of brainiacs figure out and outrun the bad guys, and slam on the handcuffs?"

"Nothing like a pushy mother." Sarah was laughing, totally surprised. "Folks, I don't know anything about this, at all." And Lynsey struggled to remember what exactly she had said now. Why was Sarah apologizing?

Fausto went on, "Well, if she'll consider it, she has my support. Lynsey, all y'all. My thanks. And, stay well."

Shirley stood. She spread her hands and her end of the white ribbon. "I love you, each of you. Especially you, Lynsey, sooo happy to see you all safe, at home. Well, I guess Faust's news will cause some little tiny ruckus around Roeller County, if anybody even notices,"—Faust shouted, "Hey now!"—"and by the way," Shirl said, "Sarah. Do it! You'd be sweeter than this old grouch"— and Faus muttered, "Hey, I'm *sweet!*"

Shirl went on, "You know, maybe you don't, I have been trying to read Isiah, I always say, 'since 2006.' It's really been since 1996.

Faus rolls his eyes every time I start,"—Faus shouted out, "Next thing I hear is Shirl snoring, I mean she's *lightly* snoring"—and Shirl, ignoring him, continued: "I'm not talkin' to him; I'm talking to my friends—but this stuck with me, right now, COVID, strange year of trouble, and new things. Ok, here we go, Isaiah 45:22: 'Turn to me and be safe—or *saved*—all the ends of the earth, for I am God, there is no other…'" She sat, her head hidden in Faus's hug. The ribbons danced.

Preston was all but embracing Cinnah, his two-step partner, and apparent soulmate. Lynsey sniffed. Their bright blue and lavender ribbons were twisted up. Some guests were directing Lynsey's attention to Gina. Inside the house, four generations: Melissa, Deidra, Gina, and the baby. Melissa was holding the baby, and they could see Gina doing a soundless, graceful slow-dance for Lynsey and her guests. Lynsey could see *Hollis*. "There. That's my boy," she tried to say, as she waved at him.

She looked up in surprise to hear an older man saying, "I hope you all have met Cinnah Shelton. She works for a news agency that focuses on Texas, and she's not only smart, she is wise." It flashed through Preston's mind to say that makes her a *wiseass* and a *smarty pants*, but he held back "And, like Mother"—Lynsey sat up, alert—"she's a writer. Some day she'll put all our stories into, well, what?" He smiled upon his wife-to-be.

"Maybe a film, we'll be in the movies," the man was saying. Lynsey watched. Julian was talking about the movies? No, no. It was *Preston* saying, "Now, two things, her first name is Cinnah. Cinnah. Just Cinnah, and—as you've heard—her last name soon will be Gerardi. Not sure if that's such a good thing for her but our lives will be joined. Cinnah has a great son, eight years old. Kevin. Right now they live in Belwin, in

Dell County. We're both Catholic, of sound minds, and after the wedding, we will live here on Melody Street.

"We'll be upstairs," he explained. His face briefly turned pink. Only Faust and Sarah noticed and exchanged microscopic browlifts. Was Preston blushing? Where was the cameraman? The scribes? The historian?

Cinnah, smiling, whispered to Preston, "They want to know when's the wedding?"

Preston laughed—for Preston, it was a laugh—"Tell you what?" He turned to Cinnah, took her hands. "Kevin's in online school. You can work anywhere. Your mom is set, for now. Your dad is fine. We, my family, are all crazy, but let's ask. *When* is the wedding?" No one spoke.

"Mother. When's the wedding?" Preston asked.

"June first." People were checking their calendars.

"Soon as Father Ruiz says Ok."

"Don't need a priest. Just do it."

"Next weekend."

"Where's the ring?" Faus yelled, and Preston answered, "Ring? Oh, *she* gets a ring? Ok, Cinnah, show them."

Cinnah, her mask down, smiling, held up her left hand and waved her fingers at her new friends. "Preston selected it, even got the size right. I'm happy you all could be here and please come to the wedding, *whenever* it is."

Someone called out, "First of June is a Monday."

"Mother," Preston asked, "a date for the wedding?"

"Saturday, June sixth, don't change it for nothin' at all."

Lynsey was wondering: Preston's about to be somebody's husband? And have an eight-year-old little boy around. Kevin? So. "Good deal," Lynsey told herself. It would be fun to have a boy clunking up and down the stairs. Or, he can run the elevator. My fool eyes have been so dry today. Hard to move. Like *crank, crank.* Like I need a crank. Going blind. And now what? A blinding pain, a *greep,* behind my forehead. I like Cinnah. Her mom has the big A. I been waitin' for it, Lord, the big A. Or the big C. Cancer. John Wayne beat it. Heart of Jesus, help. This pain is horrible, horrible. Hail Mary, full of grace. Gina is home. Shirley, she's not well. God, give her grace, *grapes.* And help CE, Cora. Forgive her, almighty Lord, for killin' them boys. Give her comfort. She was protecting people. I forgive them, Jesus. Noe Alejandro, and the big one, Cesar. He came to the house that day— right? He's the one. What if I'd hired him? Helped them. Forgive me. Both dead. Oh, now Mary is dancing. Hail Mary, help me keep silent, this pain. Yuri, Hollis, help me. I could cry. *Sniff.* Will not. Want to live. Red Clay, comin' to see me. I see JoJo. She's my daughter. Just older than Sarah, the baby. *J'aime* JoJo. She needs to watch her butt. Big as tractor.

JoJo, having already decreed guests should simply leave, whenever, no big farewells, was now passing around historically correct sized boxes of Cracker Jacks. Only the sheriff and his wife were still here, and the family. This had turned out well and JoJo congratulated herself.

When Lynsey accepted her box of Cracker Jacks, she motioned to Sarah, please open it. With her box open, her ribbons still under tight control, Lynsey dumped the Cracker Jacks out over the floor of the back porch.

"*Mother,*" Sarah cried out, "why did you do that?"

"Prize," Lynsey muttered, pulling her mask off and stashing it under her bottom. Frowning, shoveling at the spilled sticky popcorn with one foot, she struggled to say. "Find the prize. Prize for you."

Lynsey clutched the arms of her chair and screeched, "*Just help me look for the damn ring. I need, give to Sarah.*" Lynsey wanted her daughter rewarded for being been an ecstatic cop for how long, keepin' Houston safe from explosions, like happened in Texas City. "That scared us to death," she wanted to say. It was 1947, April, like this month, and Mother, and Daddy, they had us pray for the poor burned-up people. I didn't know, but they had once considered moving to Texas City. It was special to them. Texas City. *Shee.* Imagine.

Her voice steady, Lynsey pleaded, "No, no explosions. Please, find Sarah's prize. She gets the Cracker Jack." She bent down searching the scattered trail. Sarah, breaking social distancing, scooted over, put her arms around her mother and, making her sit up a bit, hugged her, ever so gently. Preston, bringing Cinnah close with him, joined Sarah in the hug. After three heart beats, he let go of Cinnah's hand so she could be free and he sank down at his mother's side. His heart, his insides, ached to hold her, be as one with her, but the only part of her free and available that he dared touch were her hands, still wrapped in ribbons. Gently he removed the colors and handed them to Sarah. He held his mother's hands in his, and thought about the hand-on-hand game his parents laughed about the day they met. He touched her shoulder, lightly as a breath, left side. Lynsey whispered, "Not hurt, just *dot* tired. Silly damn dots. Why don't we all just lie down?" Someone, Sarah, brought Pres' a chair, so mother and son sat face-to-face on the veranda.

"In just a little while, Mother, Sarah is going to get you changed into a nightgown they, Sarah and Cinnah, bought for you. It's that color you like."

"I like? *Lilac?*"

"I think so. In just a few minutes—we're going to put you in the bed and *cover you up*. Preston winked at her and said, "Mrs. Zee," and Lynsey, puzzled but pleased, agreed, "Mrs. Zee."

"Gina and the baby are going home with Deidra," Preston said and Lynsey nodded. He told her that Faus had gone out and that the girls were fixing up her bed. "Your room. You'll love it."

"What? Why?" Lynsey asked, and he answered that Faust had gone to the store to buy more yellow roses and whiskey, and she said, "Oh, boy. I need me some whiskey. But why? Listen, it's *Preston*, right? I have been trying to remember. Now, listen. Fausto needs to know this, and you, and Justin, and those *disco pisco* guys Cora likes. PTSD folks. Tell them. It's verified: Captain Willard called in the air strike."

All Preston could do was try not to smile. "People still argue about the end of that movie. Old *Apocalypse Now*, did he call it in or not," he said and she widened her eyes, saying, "Well, he did it. Goodbye, my honey."

Preston felt funny, not sad. He always got a kick out of his mother when she got wound up. "I'll tell 'em," he said. "No worry. Now let's see who is going to spend the night. Repeat after me, Melissa? *Melissa.* Cora? *Cora.* Shirley and Faus? *Faus and Shirley.* Ok? They're going to stay here with us tonight, yes? Like when X and his kids or Jitterbug ladies would stay nights. We heard snoring from all corners of the house. You'd tell us boys, 'Don't look at the ladies snoring.' Remember?"

She smiled at the shared memory but was leery of tonight's plan. "Well, sure. Sins of the eyes, but did you boys lust after *them* old women? Lord, mercy. Now tell me, what the heck is happening? Ok. Who's on first?"

"Who's on second."

"Ok, then. Who's on second, fine. Now you said, Melissa's staying, again. She's always stayin' and Cora too? I never thought we'd have a pajama party together, but, see here, Melissa married my son and Cora killed Noe and Cesar. We have a bond, you see? Sometimes I call Cora CE, and I heard you loud and clear about Faus and Shirley. And the whiskey, oh boy. And the roses." Preston, surprised, was trying to keep up.

"May I say, I want you to know it's Ok if Cinnah stays. You know, you are going to need her and someday it will be catty-whompus and you'll stay at her momma's house. And another thing, promise me you'll be like a father and a son to Fausto, after Shirley goes to heaven. He has problems, questions about Vietnam." Now tears were blinding Preston's eyes. She whispered, "Ok, you better tell me, if there's been a bad explosion in San Mateo? Is that really why people need to stay?"

"No, no explosion, they just want to stay, to be close to you, like a party. Thanks to you, we have enough beds."

"Ok, mind wandering, sorry. Tell me again, who is staying over—Cinnah?"

Preston nodded and told her, "Shirley and Faust, Melissa, and Cora. Shall we go out unto the highways and byways and drag them in by the neck?"

"No, twenty-nine or however many you said is enough, but tell me why? Has there been an explosion in San Mateo, and people need a safe place?"

"No explosions," he said. "But, we have the beds, we could bed down Atilla and the Huns, the entire enemy armies of the Confederate *and* the Union troops."

Lynsey laughed and said, "Quit it, you can't bed down Confederate soldiers, they will arrest your ass. I saw it on the TV. Watch what you say on the cell phone, promise me. They're taping you. So much hate. It was never this bad in our country, ever before. You know, poor old Faus still suffers from Viet Nam. You've got to hep him. He's my oldest son. Get it worked out. I would be happy to have him safe and livin' in this house *again*. But I'm talking about *now*. Right now. Do we have enough beds *today*?"

He said, "Do we ever."

His mother calculated, "With clean sheets, all of them?"

Preston shrugged slightly. "Clean enough," he said and they shared a naughty grin.

"Oh, I forgot," he said. "Squad Two is coming tomorrow and I'll hunt up our pastor to bring you Communion, if he's not missing."

"Is he?" she asked. "Still missing? Have they *looked*?"

Preston said, "They have indeed, 'They seek him here they seek him there, they seek him every where.'"

Lynsey spit it out, "Those *Frenchies*, they can't find nuthin'—I forgot, who they're looking for?"

"The Scarlet Pimpernel."

"That's some kinda *beer.* I thought you meant the priest."

"Father O'Connor?"

"*Flannery* O'Connor?" Lynsey asked aghast.

Preston admitted, "You know, I never *got* her"—there was a noise, a banging inside the house; voices. Faust was back with roses and whiskey. And a suitcase. And news.

"Yeah, you're right," Lyns' agreed, "Flannery was kind of grim, is that the word? Now they say she's racist. Seems like she wrote about white trash a lot, like she was kind of in *luv* with Georgia white trash, but I doubt that gal ever knew any real white trash, like us. Her family raised *peacocks.* And her people, you know, they weren't real. Fiction writers must be partly insane, right? What do ya think, young man? Insane? Twisted? Liars. But old Flannery was right about one thing: 'A Good Man Is Hard to Find.'"

"I'll say. The Marines even used to look for him." Preston explained, "Not the Scarlet Pimpernel, a few good men. A good man, maybe one."

"*Marines. Hm,* some other boy we know was going, I forget. Pray for him. But absolutely. Carry on. Now listen, Flannery never married. Like my girl Sarah," Lynsey said sadly. "There's talk about canonizing her, makin' her a saint."

"Sarah?" Preston asked shocked and she slapped her hand at him, laughing. She had a liking for bad boys.

Preston's mind kept reliving that day. Meeting Cinnah, the best thing of 2020, or of his life. (He had to remember to speak in romantic exaggerations.) Except that same "Cinnah day"— two bastards had wanted to kill Lynsey Gerardi.

Preston didn't drink, but lately he had been slugging it down, as needed. Right now he needed. He had been told to focus on "The Good." Cinnah and Kevin. New life. But in his gut, he nurtured anger. For a month, for all this 2020 nightmare, a continuous flawed moment until the *now*, a bitter lesson, the terrible news flash, the reality that goes beyond him and his mother: The elderly truly are the *oh, well*, the toss-away population. He wanted it known. Truth is, wherever you live, you can expect terror attacks, small ones, tiny, subtle, isolated, individual, as cruel as Hitler's oven– these attacks on the elderly, and massively on their twin, the unborn who can't defend themselves. Preston took a breath. Generally he avoided preaching, better to show than to tell, and he taunted himself, "Then what am I?"

He had never known anyone as directly, as deeply, as he did his mother; he had spied on her, laughed, been rude and distant. Working out his guilt, it wasn't just a way to absolve himself. Something must change. This youth cult. Throwaways, anybody over 50, or 65, over some very changeable age.

Sarah was back from crying and gabbing with the women. *Women*. Would he ever get used to it? A houseful of women? She pulled up a chair for herself. By some standards the brother and sister, son and daughter, were already irrelevant. Preston, his life just beginning, was no youngster, and Sarah, county sheriff?

Cancer, over-the-hill. But with Cinnah—they might join forces. Really work for elder needs and rights. This time.

"Talk about the irony of it, Mother," he said, half-amused, self-pleased. "No, not ironing, *irony.*"

"Pretty boy like you, you never touched a damn iron in your whole existential," his mother said. "Who are you anyhow?"

"Obviously, a total jerk," he said.

"What?" she cried out, hurt. "I say you're a sweetie."

Preston sighed. All this time, the hellfire lessons she left to her readers—"That is," he realized, "to me and Sarah, no one else"—Ok, it was all just coo-coo stuff, off-the-wall, but majestic, reasonable. It was time to tell her, face-to-face. And then to do something about it.

He took a deep breath. "I am going to tell you something, Mother, about your journals," and Lynsey snapped, "Journals! Burn 'em! *Who cares*? But, if something happens, please, the new ones, pull 'em down from the sky, the cloud, send them to Mr. Red Clay. Mr. Wallace Clay. Absolutely, send 'em to all my readers and if you need anything else, young fella, 'Just ask Preston.'"

Preston laughed. *"Mother,"* he said. "Listen. I'm admitting it. I have been reading your journals since I was a kid, for fifty-plus years. Sometimes Sarah read 'em as well." Sarah, now scooting her own chair as close as possible to her mother, began fixing Lynsey's snowy white curls.

Preston's voice was clear and kind above the evening birds cooing at each other, "But I am the main one, I have been tricking you—"

Lynsey lifted her face to him. Her eyes were stiff as paper, and she could hardly hear, not over the roar of the ocean, and all those wild birds.

He started again, "I apologize, but reading your journal, every word you wrote. It was so much fun. It was great. I learned everything. I didn't need college."

He laughed a little and she tried to return a semi-smile. "You know," he said, "I was always bustin' to tell those *bizi badies* who asked why I live with my mother, that, if I moved out, I wouldn't get to read her journals. It was me, all this time, driving you crazy. I apologize."

Sitting face-to-face with his mother, he lay his head on her shoulder. And she rocked him slightly, sadly, back and forth. With a shock, she realized she could not hear at all, not the whoosh of the ocean, not the birds, no. There was just pure silence.

She had not heard a word of the young man's speech. She did not know who he was, this young fellow crying on her shoulder, but she patted him kindly and murmured and purred to him and tried to say, "I know. I know, sweetheart. Don't worry. It's all just fine."

And with a glance, a turn of her eyes, she looked up and saw a dark-haired girl and a blonde one, smiling so sweetly at her and she wondered: Who are these girls, so pretty? Then she was lifted up, so very surprised to be as young as they, all of them, even her sons, some little girls, and all the elders, Poppy & Mother, nurses, *angels*, & the old soldiers, more boys and girls, Ben Weaver, wonderful Red Clay, powerful & urgent in the Saverne sunlight, all those dear precious readers. I *see* y'all now. And Daddy, & Vin O'Quin, and Julian, young & trim. And Preston, who never left me, and

Sarah, the baby. Lynsey tried to say, "It *was* fun. Thank you," but couldn't. And the young man, the girls. *Wow.* They are just lovely. And she wished she'd known them better, as they—in the golden evening air—just hugged & hugged her, for the longest time.

It was to be Lynsey Ann's last hug.

Roeller County, Texas
The San Mateo *Argus*

"Eyes on the news"

LYNSEY ANN BERGERON GERARDI

Sunrise: September 6, 1933 Saverne, Texas

Sunset: April 26, 2020

San Mateo, Texas

by Cinnah Shelton

Preston Michael Gerardi of San Mateo, and his sister Sarah Madaline Gerardi, also of San Mateo and formerly of Houston, are deeply saddened to announce the death of their mother, Lynsey Ann Bergeron Gerardi. Mrs. Gerardi died peacefully of natural causes while surrounded by family and friends on April, the 25th.

April is the cruelest month, breeding lilacs out of the dead land, mixing memory and desire, stirring dull roots with spring rain.

T.S. Eliot. *The Waste Land*

Sarah Gerardi said about her mother, "Because of our sorrow and incredible sense of loss, we join with you, all of you who are suffering during this time of the Coronavirus, from illness, anxiety and loss of job or income, or the death of someone you love. So while our mother died neither from COVID nor from any lingering wounds from a violent physical assault one month ago, my brother and I agree she would approve our use of John Donne's very famous words from what he called "Holy Sonnet 10," or you may recall it from high school as, "Death, be not proud."

"In the poem we might say that John Donne argues with a Mister Death, telling him, don't think you are so important. No, you only come around at the worst times, and in the end, Donne tells death, 'You will die.' How? Let's look around us today: Life goes on, babies are born, the sun comes up. And we who remain, even after the death of someone we love, we want to visit, talk, finish what we were working on just yesterday. Life moves forward, even with the death of someone we still want with us. But in the distance, with history as our guide, we too can see life is more powerful and in heaven, at the end of time, there will be no more death. Life is stronger, and ongoing. The death of someone you love and need is only a step—a different format—in the eternal struggle to send life on and into the great perpetual beyond, and that is not Death. Death dies."

Lynsey Ann Gerardi, a lifelong and enduring Catholic, was owner and developer of Jitterbug, Inc., the Bergeron Agency, and several Gerardi's Day-and-Night Senior Care Centers, all businesses that benefit the elderly. She was the mother of three living children, Sarah Madeline and Preston Michael, and his wife-to-be Cinnah Shelton of Belwin, Texas, and also Lynsey's daughter Jewel Gerardi Glendening of Spain and Scotland. Lynsey's only grandchild, Rosa Glendening Iglesias, and her great grandson Juan Carlos Iglesias, are living in Tarragona, Catalonia, Spain.

Lynsey is preceded in death by her parents, her husband Julian Peter and two sons, Yuri "George" and Hollis Edward.

Because of the restrictions of COVID-19, the family will attend a private Mass with a private burial service at St. Matthew's Cemetery, San Mateo. Lynsey Ann asked those who wish "to kindly do something," to remember her, simply to have kind thoughts on the day you read this, that you save your money for a rainy day, and avoid "donations" to large non-profit corporations. But if you still want to do something, she hoped you will buy yourself any book you like online, or buy plants. She suggested "chicks and hens," easy care succulents which are said to live forever. Pray for us as we face this tasking sorrow, pray for the happy repose of our mother's soul, pray for our country, and for each other.

www.ingramcontent.com/pod-product-compliance
Lightning Source LLC
Chambersburg PA
CBHW020639110726
47899CB00002B/824